*'Pictures of perfection, as you know,
make me sick and wicked . . .'*

Jane Austen, Letter to Fanny Knight,
March 23, 1816

CRIME
AND
PREJUDICE

JULIA L. MILLER

Crime and Prejudice

Published by Wild Card Books
Copyright © 2024 Julia L. Miller

Cover design & typesetting by riverdesignbooks.com

ISBN: 978-1-7637051-0-4 (Audio)
ISBN: 978-1-7637051-1-1 (Ebook)
ISBN: 978-1-7637051-2-8 (Paperback)
ISBN: 978-1-7637051-3-5 (Hardback)

Contents

Chapter 1

Elizabeth Darcy – First Impressions

I did not intend to start a riot, but I am proud that some reference to our story appears in the records of the Old Bailey law-courts. I hope it will be an inspiration for women everywhere. This was the charge:

> ELIZABETH DARCY and GEORGIANA DARCY were indicted for that they, on the 6th of April, riotously and tumultuously did assemble for the purpose of breaking in pieces the premises, with one hundred other persons, of Mr. Joshua Heaven.

After my marriage to my dear Fitzwilliam, I was very happy, but I faced an unusual conundrum. Where before, my days were spent answering to my mother's many whims or watching over my younger sisters, now my time was my own, and I spent much of it in the library with my husband. I was not a great reader before I came to Pemberley, but old Mr. Darcy's collection is very grand, and there are not one, but two copies of that most interesting treatise, Mary Wollstonecraft's *A Vindication of the Rights of Woman*. Although I do not agree with all her sentiments, this is a book I have long studied, and to which I allude frequently in my dealings with the male sex. When I declined Mr. Collins's proposal of marriage, for instance, I assured him that, in Mary Wollstonecraft's words, I was a 'rational creature', and spoke only the truth in refusing his offer of matrimony. Though he persisted in misunderstanding me, that was none of my doing.

I was not surprised to find that Fitzwilliam, unlike Mr. Collins, had read Miss Wollstonecraft's *Vindication*, and we spent many spirited evenings debating her words. We concurred with her observation that ladies in society are expected to be patient, docile and good-humoured, like my sister Jane, and are seldom seen to exert themselves physically. I disagreed, however, with her statement that no vigorous exercise of the intellect was demanded in exhibiting these virtues. I have, on occasion, employed all my mental faculties in attempting to appear civil to the likes of Mr. Collins. Fitzwilliam only laughed, and said he was never mistaken in my character, but it was a shame that a woman's strength of intellect should be sacrificed to the acquiring of accomplishments such as singing and sewing. Then I teased him about our conversation at Netherfield Hall, when he enumerated so many qualities of an accomplished woman that I wondered at him knowing any at all. He drew me to him and said that from the moment he first saw me at Netherfield, he realised that I far surpassed all his expectations.

I enjoyed our discussions, and yet I was anxious for my reading to carry into some practical application. I longed to do further study and develop my ideas by discussing them with a greater number of scholars. Fitzwilliam's university friend Adam Sedgwick visited us sometimes from Cambridge, where he was now a professor of geology, and he praised my spirit of enquiry and told me of women such as Miss Mary Anning in Lyme Regis, who conducted scientific work of their own. This led me to wonder why I should not attend a university, as Fitzwilliam had done, and increase my knowledge of different subjects. To my surprise, Fitzwilliam was rather disparaging of university education.

'There are some capital men like Sedgwick,' he said, 'but many of the teaching fellows at Cambridge are ignorant, and many undergraduates spend their time, as Wickham did, in loose living and debauchery. Only a small number of men who attended Cambridge with me have attained to any position of consequence. Most of them have become country parsons. My dear, a university degree is not worth as much as a fine mind, and that you already have.'

'And fine eyes too?' I teased him.

'Very fine,' he said. 'And you use them to make the keenest observations. Why do you not write a novel about what you have observed, and the prejudices that you overcame in becoming mistress of Pemberley? I wager it would be of more interest and help to other women than any number of treatises on the book of Leviticus you might compose as an undergraduate at Cambridge. You could write to inspire other women who must deal with difficulties in their own homes.' He turned to his sister. 'Is that not so, Georgiana?'

'Very true,' she said. 'I would like to read your first impressions of all those around you, my dearest Lizzy, and to see for myself if they were correct. Would there not be many women who would find hope in your story, and instruction in dealing with difficult relatives?'

'Then maybe I will write a novel detailing my impressions of life before and after my marriage,' I said. 'But first I must see your own seat of learning, Fitzwilliam, my love. How can I settle to write in our library at Pemberley if I have not seen some of the country's great university libraries?'

Some weeks later, Georgiana, Fitzwilliam and I visited Cambridge, where we stayed at the Pickerel Inn on Magdalene-street, near Fitzwilliam's old college. It is the oldest inn in Cambridge, well situated near the river, and we had a pleasant walk around the town. The buildings are magnificent, and the college libraries made me exceedingly envious. Why do not women have the right to attend these places of learning? It is not through any want of intellect. But I looked in vain for a female scholar; all those clad in academic garb were men. That night, I made a vow to myself—I would agitate for women's education and equality; I would write a novel for Georgiana; and I would attend the University of Cambridge.

We had three days to spend in the town, and Fitzwilliam introduced us to some excellent college fellows who had studied there with him, including Hensleigh Wedgwood, whose cousin, Caroline Darwin, was visiting from Shrewsbury with her parents. Caroline Darwin had long been an advocate for women's education, and Hensleigh was vociferous in support of my project. Their friend Adam Sedgwick seemed amused rather than enthused, but he allowed that women such as Mary Anning could make a great contribution to the scientific cause.

Caroline, Georgiana and I met the next day to take a turn about the centre of the town.

'I am very glad to see you,' said Caroline. 'Our cause has many women supporters, although some men are either disdainful or openly against us, and there is one man in the town who is notoriously antagonistic. His name is Joshua Heaven, and he runs a bookshop near the Senate House at the end of King's-parade. You will meet him later. But first let us visit the Parker Library at Corpus Christi College. The librarian is a friend of mine, and he will shew us the library's prized collection of illuminated manuscripts.'

She led us down King's-parade to Corpus Christi, where we crossed the College court-yard and arrived at the great wooden door to the Parker Library. It was open, and we ascended the staircase and entered the reading room. I was delighted to see the ancient books and manuscripts, but we had no sooner taken a volume from the shelves than a man descended on us. He looked like a very old bat, his voluminous black gown swirling behind him like a pair of wings, and his white hair spurting around his head like a swarm of elderly bees. In vain did Caroline explain she had visited the library many times before; he would not permit us to enter without a letter of introduction or the presence of a fellow of the College.

'You see,' said Caroline, as we walked back along King's-parade. 'Many of our attempts at self-education are met in this way. That is why we have determined to march here in procession, to challenge the men and demand the right of women to study at the university on an equal footing. We have formed a group called the Women's Initiative for Science and Education. Will you join us in our protest?'

Indeed I would. There was almost no cause dearer to my heart than to see women's education advanced and to be allowed myself to study in this seat of learning. I was all the more determined when we entered Mr. Heaven's bookshop after our attempt to visit the Parker Library had failed. In vain did I look on Mr. Heaven's shelves for any volume by Mary Wollstonecraft, or indeed, by any other lady. I enquired of the owner himself why there might be a dearth of women writers, and his reply was as forthright as Lady Catherine's might have been, and as uneducated as Mr. Collins's would undoubtedly have proved.

'We have no need of women writers,' said Mr. Heaven. 'Women do not read any thing of substance, and men do not wish to read any thing written by a woman.'

Then he settled his glasses on his nose and sat down behind the counter, ignoring us. We left the shop quickly. I would not have given him my custom if his had been the only bookshop in the country. After that encounter, my mind was decided. I would join the Women's Initiative for Science and Education, my WISE sisters.

Fitzwilliam, when I told him, said we sounded like Macbeth's witches, and asked me if I did not despise broom-sticks as representing typical women's work. But he said it so humorously I could not be cross with him. Georgiana was still in awe of him, but beginning to understand I could take liberties with him as his wife that she still felt unable to take with him as her elder brother. She was at first apprehensive as to what Fitzwilliam would say about her joining the procession, but I encouraged her to think for herself.

'For,' I said, 'you cannot fight for freedom if you are too fearful of gaining your brother's approbation before you take a step. Tease him a little. You will find he is game.'

'Then I will join,' she said. 'And what of your other sisters? Will they take part?'

I thought this an excellent idea, and I wrote at once to Jane. She was timid, but held absolutely to the rights of women to an education. She was unable to walk with us, as she was expecting a happy event at any moment, but she would be with us in spirit. It took me many weeks to contact Lydia, who was visiting her friend Mrs. Forster in Brighton, but she wrote me eventually that it would be 'a lark' and she would join us if she could. Kitty was unable to come, but she understood our proposal and was behind us. I had great hopes of Mary, asking her only not to tell our mother, whose nerves could not have borne the strain. Mary wrote me that she approved our cause, but that one false step could lead to our downfall, and we should be entirely circumspect in our dealings with the less meritorious of the other sex. I took this to mean she would not join us, but I was neither surprised nor dismayed. I hoped she would find her own way in the world eventually. My Aunt Gardiner, however, was enthusiastic in her support. Georgiana raised the subject with Caroline Bingley and Mrs. Hurst, and although Mrs.

Hurst had no desire to mix with women whose connections were so far beneath her own, Miss Bingley thought it an admirable plan and said she would endeavour to be present. I did not know whether this was a display of her habitual insincerity, or a keen desire to further the cause of women.

Caroline Darwin, Georgiana and I began our WISE campaign by gathering signatures from the wives of famous scholars, and women who were free thinkers. We were pleased to encounter many such women and girls, in London and Cambridge and elsewhere. After weeks of preparation, we planned our Cambridge procession for early April. We would march down King's-parade waving banners, and call on the university authorities to listen to our message and grant women the right to a university education. All we asked was to be admitted according to our own intellectual merit. We had a petition of four hundred pages of signatures, many from prominent women such as Caroline Darwin's family, with their links to the famous Wedgwoods, and Mary Wollstonecraft's daughter Mary, who told us she had written a successful book, but that it was published anonymously. You will know how successful a book it was when I tell you its name was *Frankenstein, or the Modern Prometheus*, although her name did not appear on the cover until three years after its publication.

We knew that many men were not interested in our message, but we had not envisaged that so many would oppose it. Fitzwilliam and I returned to Cambridge a week before our procession, and as the day approached, we saw posters around the town proclaiming, 'The 'Varsity for Men and Men for the 'Varsity.' I could not understand why they should feel so threatened. They even suspended an effigy of a woman wearing an undergraduate gown and mortarboard above Mr. Heaven's bookshop at the end of King's-parade, on the corner of St. Mary's-street. Georgiana was dismayed, but, as I once remarked to Fitzwilliam, my own courage is always aroused when any one tries to intimidate me, and I was ready to do battle.

We ladies met outside Queens' College. We deemed it an appropriate site to begin our procession, which would progress along historic King's-parade as far as the Senate House. We numbered around a hundred, and our male supporters marched along the edges of the road beside us. Fitzwilliam of course was there, with Jane's husband Charles and Fitzwilliam's cousin Colonel Fitzwilliam. They were joined by my Uncle Gardiner and Caroline Darwin's brothers Charles and Erasmus, as well as her cousin Hensleigh. We chanted in unison, 'University education for women!' At the same time, some men stood along the pavement shouting, 'Are women's brains the same as men's?' 'Do women have intellectual power?' 'As well admit a monkey as a woman!' Men and women thronged the streets and balconies of the shops and houses on King's-parade, and others looked down from the tower of Great St. Mary's.

As we drew nearer to the Senate House, some men began to throw eggs, confetti, grit and dirt at us. It was more violent than we had anticipated, and very abasing to those men whose masculinity was challenged at the sight of a few women wishing to be admitted to the university. One man in particular endeavoured to impede us, grinning in our faces as he walked backwards before us, extravagantly sweeping his hat and mocking us at every step. He had the smirking, arrogant face of an indolent Wickham, and I heartily wished him to a warmer place.

'I do not think we shall ever be admitted to their colleges,' said Georgiana, 'but now I do not want to go in any case. Can we not found a college for women?'

'Indeed,' I said. 'But why stop at one college, dear Georgiana? Let us have two or three, at least. Oxford has a New College. We shall start a New Hall, for women only.'

'And a college named for my brother and our cousin?' she asked.

'Certainly. A Fitzwilliam College, for both men and women!'

We had intended to nail our petition to the door of the Senate House, which was a method of protest we knew had a good precedent with Martin Luther. Alas, Cambridge was less advanced than Luther's town of Wittenberg. I heard a shout, and turned to see Caroline Darwin endeavouring to restrain Mr. Heaven, the keeper of the bookshop with the suspended female effigy, who was attempting to pull Georgiana into his shop. It was too much to bear. I had four copies of Mary Wollstonecraft's *Vindication* in my reticule, and I swung it at his head. He staggered, but was instantly back on his feet, where he was set upon by Mrs. Gardiner, Caroline and the other ladies. He lunged at them in a very ungentlemanly manner, but one pulled his hair and another hit him in the stomach, until he gave up and dashed into his shop, barring the door behind him. The crowd laughed at our boldness. This did not mean we had won the fight, however. Other men pushed forward, and still others overturned carts and started a bonfire in the market place. Officers of the law were called, and the women's names were noted down, but the men who started the disturbance ran away. It was hours before order was restored.

Some days later, we were at breakfast at Pemberley when we received a letter stating that Georgiana and I were charged with assembling for the purpose of breaking in pieces the premises, with a hundred other persons, of a Mr. Joshua Heaven. To wit, we were being indicted for rioting. I laughed at this news, for we did not intend to break any one's property, and Mr. Heaven's shop was undamaged by the riot which ensued, none of which was our doing. Fitzwilliam's brow, however, was clouded. I had not seen him look this disturbed since the news of Lydia's elopement with Wickham. I regarded him in consternation.

'You are angry,' I said.

He looked at me sternly. 'No, I am not angry, Elizabeth. I am merely disappointed.'

My heart sunk, not at his disappointment, but at his apparent return to the serious demeanour he had displayed before our engagement. I wondered, then, if my first impressions of him so long ago at Netherfield had not been correct after all, and if his apparent alteration of character was not to last now we were married. I was heavy-hearted indeed at such a thought.

Georgiana was in a flutter of nerves as he rose abruptly and left the table. 'Disappointed? Lord, that is worse than angry. Where is he going?' she asked me.

I did not know. I sincerely hoped he had not changed, but I knew that serious circumstances could have grave consequences. I had but lately learned from Caroline Darwin that a husband was held legally liable for his wife's actions. Perhaps this smirch on the name of Darcy was too much for him to countenance. We watched as a little time later, dressed in his finest outfit, he strode to the stables and rode away.

Georgiana spent the day in a fit of discomfort and would not settle to any thing. We did not hear from Fitzwilliam for two days. On the third day, my sister Jane and her husband came in their carriage with their new baby, a delightful little girl with all of Jane's good looks and Charles's easy temper.

'Here is a fine state of affairs,' said Charles, throwing himself into a chair and laughing. 'My wife's sister a law-breaker, her face on wanted posters in three counties.'

'My dear,' said Jane, 'you exaggerate. You will scare Georgiana. Their faces are not on posters. And are we not all law-breakers, to a greater or lesser extent?'

I smiled to myself. Jane is so good and kind, she could never break a law, though she would always speak in defence of others.

'I do not know,' I said. 'I am sure you are not a criminal, Jane. But I know we did nothing wrong. We only performed our duty in protesting for the rights of women; and it is useless to agonise over that which cannot be changed.'

'Well said,' said Charles. 'You see, Jane? Did I not say Lizzy would not be anxious? Lizzy, my wife is chiding me for the blows Darcy and I landed on Wickham's old friends in the scrum at the riot. I confess, I haven't had so much fun since I was at school. You must incite another riot again soon. It will liven us all up.'

'My dear,' said Jane, smiling and reaching for his hand, 'you have forgotten the point of the protest. It was not to provide an excuse for the men to fight, but to promote the cause of women.'

'Well, well,' said Charles. 'Why should we not do both? For my part, I never saw so many intelligent women all together, or so many ignorant men asking to have their noses put out of joint.'

This was a very violent observation indeed on the part of Mr. Bingley, but I liked him all the better for it. He and Jane were taken advantage of by their servants at every turn, as my father had predicted before their wedding, and they were both so compliant that I was glad to see him taking the initiative and defending his wife, just as I was glad to see her standing up for the rights of her sex.

'And what will you do with this indictment?' he asked. 'Will you go to court?'

'I think we must,' I said. 'But it is unjust. We did not incite violence, and this man's property was not destroyed. We shall tell the judge.'

'And we shall be there as witnesses,' said Charles. 'Upon my soul, this Joshua Heaven must be a very stupid kind of man if he thinks he will get away with this. What does Darcy say?'

'You may ask him yourself,' said Georgiana, who had scarce left her window seat since her brother departed. Now she came running to the table, her cheeks red and her eyes sparkling, her vigil at an end. 'Here he is!'

She rushed to the door and embraced him. He looked a little tired, but his face had that determined aspect I recognised from when he left me in Lambton after Lydia's disappearance with Wickham. My spirits rose.

'I am sorry I did not tell you my plans,' he said. 'I did not know if I would be successful, and I did not want to raise your hopes only to disappoint them. But I have spoken to my attorney, and all will be well. We shall go to the court and you will not be found guilty.'

'As we are not!' I exclaimed.

'How do you know what will happen?' asked Jane. 'What if you are not successful?'

'I have it on very good authority that there is a precedent for our case,' said Fitzwilliam.

That was all he would say.

After dinner, Fitzwilliam and I retired to bed and I pressed him for further details. He told me that if his attorney's advice were correct, we would be found not guilty of any charges.

'And if we are found guilty?' I asked.

He looked grave. 'The consequences would be very serious. Transportation to Australia would be the kindest sentence.'

'The kindest? Good God. What is the worst?'

'The death penalty.'

Never before had I been in such a situation. I had intended only to promote the rights of my sex. Now I had exposed

Georgiana to a terrible ordeal that might meet with a truly dreadful fate. I knew now why Fitzwilliam had looked so grave. But no one was injured during the riot, and I determined to find witnesses who would affirm that we did not start any violence.

Caroline Darwin and I rallied our supporters, and there were many in Cambridge, both men and women, prepared to testify that the violence was wholly on the part of the men who burned the wooden carts.

On the day of our trial, Fitzwilliam said we should have a good meal at the Pickerel Inn to fortify ourselves. We tried to eat a hearty breakfast, as condemned persons are said to do, but we could touch nothing more than a cup of tea. Georgiana was unaware of the possible sentences, but she was pale with dread, and I, who understood more, was hard pressed to maintain a steady countenance before her.

Only Georgiana and I were named on the indictment, but our dear WISE sisters came to support us. The charge of rioting was a very serious one, and although Fitzwilliam had told me his strategy, I was not entirely confident we would win our case. I wanted to protest our innocence, with evidence from many witnesses that we had not provoked Mr. Heaven or caused any material damage, but I hoped Fitzwilliam's strategy might work, and, as it was so simple, I agreed we should try it first.

We took the carriage to the law-court, although it was not far to walk, and the roads were thronged with men and women come to hear the outcome and to jeer or cheer, according to their prejudices. I saw the bat from the Parker Library, looking fierce, and next to him, Professor Adam

Sedgwick and Caroline Darwin with her cousin and brothers, applauding and wishing us well.

Fitzwilliam, Georgiana and I entered the court.

The clerk read the charge:

> ELIZABETH DARCY and GEORGIANA DARCY are indicted for that they, on the 6th of April, riotously and tumultuously did assemble for the purpose of breaking in pieces the premises, with one hundred other persons, of Mr. Joshua Heaven.

The witness, Mr. Heaven, was produced. He glared at us as he took his place. Then the judge asked him his Christian name.

'Joshua George Heaven,' he answered.

The judge looked at his papers. 'It says here in the indictment that your name is Joshua Heaven. There is no George here.' He turned to the constable. 'The women are not guilty. You consequently must acquit the prisoners.'

There was a great murmuring and muttering in the court, but a stern look from the judge was sufficient to disperse the assembly.

I could scarce believe it. After all our preparation and anxious waiting, it came down to this—an error in the writing of Joshua Heaven's name. Was this how laws were decided and justice meted out in our land? What of those who were guilty and wrongfully pardoned, or those who were not guilty but were unjustly sentenced? Those who were transported to the other side of the world because of a mistake or a false testimony? I had never attended a court of law before, and I had no idea a case could proceed in this way and be overturned on such a triviality.

Georgiana and I left the court-room, and women swarmed around us to offer their congratulations. Georgiana was almost too stunned to comprehend what had passed, and I was laughing and crying in turns.

Fitzwilliam was reserved, as always, but I knew how happy he was by the way he put his arms around me and Georgiana and kissed us alternately on the cheek. Charles was jubilant and threw his hat in the air, while Jane embraced us and wept and embraced us again.

We adjourned to the Pickerel Inn and ate a hearty meal. This time we did not stint, and Georgiana's cheeks were flushed with wine and excitement.

'My dear,' I asked Fitzwilliam, when we were toasting our victory, 'how did you know you would be successful?'

'I made some enquiries in Cambridge,' he said, 'and I discovered that Heaven has a middle name.'

'But why should this detail matter?' I asked. 'Surely any number of criminals might be pardoned on such a technicality?'

'It matters not a jot to the severity of the crime,' said Fitzwilliam. 'But during my studies at Cambridge, I learned of precedents such as this. Three people were acquitted of a charge of rioting but a few years ago, because the witness's details differed by only the middle name. And by heaven, the same is true of your bookshop owner.'

'Then,' I said, 'your impressions of Cambridge are not entirely reliable. You see, you did learn something, in spite of your protestations to the contrary.'

'That is true,' he said. 'And when you study here, you will learn things too.'

'Alas, I am afraid that may not be for many years yet,' I answered.

~~~

I was disappointed that our protest had met with such resistance, but it is not in my nature to dwell on unavoidable vexations and so increase them. I was confident of having performed my duty, and I would continue to perform it. A few years later, Caroline Darwin invited me to visit her brother Charles when he went up to Christ's College, and we attended his matriculation ceremony at the Senate House, presided over by Professor Adam Sedgwick. It was an impressive occasion, and I vowed to do all I could to have women included in the list of those matriculating, and to join in their number.

I knew such a moment would not come quickly, however, and so I settled down in the library at Pemberley to pen my novel. I thought, on reflection, that my impressions of life before and after marriage might be too narrow a subject, and since I did not know all my friends' and family's secrets, I determined to ask the principal actors to write their own narratives. I hoped my own encounter with crime might stimulate them to admit to their own less than perfect natures. To my great astonishment, they agreed, but only if I undertook not to publish the manuscript for a considerable length of time, that none might be disgraced by the candour of their admissions. We are not a religious family, but I think it came as a relief to many of them to confess their own misdemeanours.

My collection of stories has thus been many years in the writing, but you may judge for yourself if your own first impressions of my friends and family, gained from whatever sources you may have encountered, were at all correct.

CHAPTER 2

MR. COLLINS – HER LADYSHIP DISPOSES

I write these remembrances for you to read upon my demise, my dear Anne, to shew I am for ever sensible of the warmest gratitude towards the person who brought me into the parish. I trust no obloquy will fall on your dear father when you read this narrative. Indeed, I write this account only to explain the circumstances of what may possibly have puzzled you when you were not more profitably occupied with music and art and the thousand little industries to which your fair hand was turned by your much beloved mother, may she rest in peace. You will see, I hope, that the estate is now entirely yours, since your dear father can never return.

How well I recall the day I first visited your home, and embarked on what must surely be one of the most agreeable of vocations, with the added blessing of the most admirable of patronesses. Her ladyship had condescended to invite myself and another young man, Mr. Stephens, to her magnificent dwelling, to discuss the living which had but recently fallen vacant, the former incumbent having died not a fortnight since. I had taken orders only a few weeks previously and was greatly honoured to be chosen for such a distinction, and to be collected from the post in one of her ladyship's three carriages. As we rounded the churchyard, where a freshly dug grave reminded us of the shortness of our earthly sojourn, I was overcome with emotion to see her ladyship standing on the steps of her abode, preparing to greet us. I perceived immediately that she was the sort of woman who commands the utmost deference. Her handsome mien and striking presence led me to believe at once that our intercourse would be most congenial.

Indeed, I was not mistaken, for she requested that both Mr. Stephens and I spend the night, and made sure no comfort was spared in preparing a room for me in the servants' quarters. I am not accustomed to luxury, and the small cot and closet (ingeniously fitted with shelves) were very pleasant. I spent a happy hour secluded in my room, mastering my emotions and preparing for the evening meal, and was a little surprised, on entering the dining-parlour later, to see the other candidate, Mr. Stephens, arriving from a different direction. I can only assume he lost his way in the myriad of corridors, as he seemed flushed with exertion and was still adjusting his cravat as he came into the room. Her ladyship followed soon after, and the slight rosiness in her cheeks only served to enhance her flawless complexion. Sir Lewis, who was already at the dining-table, did not smile, but his air of gravity lent distinction to all his movements. I learned that he and my lady had a daughter, yourself, whom I imagined to be no doubt as beauteous as her mother, but she was indisposed and unable to join us.

The meal was of the very finest, with seven courses, and I am not ashamed to admit that the whole affair was so delightful that I drank *two* glasses of wine, which I think, given the circumstances and the delightful company, was not overly indulgent. Her ladyship pronounced with authority on a great many matters, while his lordship sat silently, I might even say frostily, looking straight ahead and paying little attention to her ladyship's keenly intelligent observations. Perhaps for this reason, her ladyship addressed herself almost exclusively to Mr. Stephens. I may say that, unaccustomed as I am to such superb and scintillating conversation, I could but look on in awe and count my blessings at being included in such a ceremony.

After dinner, the gentlemen repaired to the library, where I counted no less than seventeen flintlocks on the walls, besides several sets of exquisitely bound sermons on the shelves. His lordship started to reminisce on his time in Portugal with Wellington, but was interrupted by the maid inviting us to make haste to the drawing-room, where her ladyship wished us to join her in a game of quadrille. Her ladyship, of course, played with consummate skill, and I was thankful to her for every fish I won and felt obliged to apologise if ever I won too many. I am in fact not very familiar with the game, but I assume Mr. Stephens played well, because her ladyship gave him many approving glances.

The evening was too short, and it was no time before her ladyship stood up to bid us good night. I made my way easily enough to my room, as her ladyship had thoughtfully provided me with a small candle, the larger candles being necessary to light the way for herself, his lordship and Mr.

Stephens, who would undoubtedly have lost his way again, since he wandered in the direction of the state bedrooms. I am sure the mistake was rectified in time, but I did not see, as I went immediately to my own comfortable room.

I am a very light sleeper, and I was awakened in the middle of the night by what sounded like a scream coming from the direction of the state rooms. After I had managed to light what remained of my candle, I determined to go and see if I could be of assistance. It was some distance from the servants' quarters to the rest of the house, and all was quiet, so there was little to guide me. Happily, at this moment I heard another sound, something like a muffled shout, and this time there was no mistaking its provenance. I hastened to the drawing-room and met there with a scene so shocking, it pains me to describe it. Before the massive fireplace (whose chimney-piece alone must have been worth many hundreds of pounds) I found Mr. Stephens. He was in a state of undress, and his eyes were staring wildly as he shouted, 'No, no, do not touch me!'

I assured him I had not the slightest intention of touching him, but he replied, 'Good God, man. Not you! I must leave at once. Stay away from her. She is insatiable!' And with that, he pulled his nightshirt closer to him, seized his candlestick and rushed from the room. I retrieved my candle stump and returned to my own accommodation.

In the morning, I learned Mr. Stephens had departed before breakfast. His lordship took a hasty meal and then went out to shoot duck, and her ladyship was nowhere to be seen. Miss Bishop, your companion, informed me that she had not seen or heard her ladyship that morning, and that you, my dear Anne, were still in your apartments at the far end of the house, as you were of a sickly constitution and still felt indisposed. The servants' quarters were so far removed from the rest of the house that once they had retired to bed they were unaware of any sound outside their own rooms, unless they were summoned by a bell in the servants' kitchen. It was my own wakefulness that had permitted me to hear the commotion during the night.

I partook of breakfast by myself, enjoying the generous provision of Bath cakes and hot chocolate, and was not discomfited at the thought of dining alone without my hostess. Indeed, I flatter myself I know something of the ways of the fairer sex, and we must make allowance for the time they spend in preparation for an evening's entertainment, especially when such an admirable woman as her ladyship had guests about whom she was so solicitous. I therefore spent the morning and afternoon in solemn study of Fordyce's *Sermons to Young Women*, not forgetting to take a little healthful exercise in the beautiful grounds. The churchyard was nearby, and while the sight of the grave freshly dug for the previous incumbent of the parish prompted me to muse once more on the shortness of life, I yet permitted myself to imagine how it would feel to become vicar of such a bountiful estate as her ladyship's.

In the evening, I found his lordship at the dinner table, and her ladyship soon joined us. I deemed it appropriate to comment on the early departure of Mr. Stephens, and to hope their sleep had not been interrupted, as mine had been, by his wild behaviour. Her ladyship did not comment, but his lordship, who is very deaf, asked me in language unfit for a lady's presence what the d*** I meant. I was therefore constrained to tell him of the state in which I had found my brother of the cloth, and I repeated his words as closely as I was able. I added that they might do well to discover and dismiss the servant to whom he had referred, and who had so clearly been stealing from the pantry. His lordship said nothing, but his colour changed and his face became a dark shade of purple. He looked at me even more frostily than he had done the previous evening, and left the table abruptly without bidding us good night. I supposed he had eaten something that disagreed with him, although the food was of course excellent. Her ladyship, however, smiled and confirmed he was indeed prone to dyspepsia.

His lordship did not return, and I spent a very pleasant hour with her ladyship, listening to her plans for the improvement of the villagers. Indeed, I admit I felt it entirely possible the living would fall to me, since the former rector had died suddenly of a heart attack and my only competitor, Mr. Stephens, had left so precipitately.

Her ladyship retired early, so I took up my candle stump and returned to my own chamber, where I pored once more over Fordyce's sermons and prepared a little all-purpose homily of my own. I find such little collections of ready words are very acceptable to the ladies. They do not want to be overtasked with matters beyond their concern, and a word in season has often proved timely in allaying their small anxieties.

After completing my task, I repaired to my bed, but alas, this night too was fated, as I had barely extinguished my candle when I again heard voices raised, once more from the direction of the main house. Anxious lest her ladyship be disturbed by quarrelsome servants, who had no place in the principal apartments after every one had retired for the night, I lit my candle stub and trod warily in pursuit of the source of the commotion.

Outside the library I halted in astonishment, for the voices were those of her ladyship and her husband.

'That is enough,' he said. 'I tell you, I will have no more of this behaviour. First a heart attack in flagrante delicto, and now the second runs away in horror. Good God, madam, pray contain yourself, or I will have you put away.'

'Never,' she replied. 'One daughter, only one daughter, and she a sickly little thing. I tell you, I want a son!'

'Then it will be none of mine, for I'll not share my bed with you again, you Jezebel!'

'How dare you, sir!' she shouted.

I heard a shot and the sound of a heavy object thudding to the ground, a table overturning and the shattering of glass. Then there was silence. So concerned was I that something untoward had happened to her ladyship, that I pushed open the door to the library. There was my lady, a flintlock in her hand, and on the Turkey carpet lay his lordship, the blood trickling from his mouth mingling with the blood flowing from his chest and forming a dark pool with the port wine from the broken decanter that lay in a thousand pieces at his side. I need not tell you how appalling this sight was. I gazed in horror until her ladyship spoke. Her handsome face looked troubled as she passed the gun to me and said in a soulful voice, 'A most unfortunate accident. His lordship was pointing the flintlock at me, and when I tried to take it from him he aimed the gun at himself and pulled the trigger.'

I perceived the truth of this at once, and my only thought was to spare her ladyship any further distress. 'What is to be done?' I asked. 'Shall I send for a doctor?'

'There is no need,' she said, 'for he is quite dead.'

She reflected and then added, 'You must bury his body in the churchyard and give him a Christian ceremony. Go. There is a spade in the outhouses, and a grave freshly dug for the last rector of our church. Poor man. He took good care of us, body and soul . . . You will place his lordship's body on the rector's coffin and seal the grave up so that no one will know.'

I saw immediately this was the best course of action. To broadcast the fact that his lordship had taken his own life in this manner would have been to provoke a scandal, and it was out of the question that any one else should see the body in the library, so I hastened to the outhouse and found the spade. Then I returned to the library and rolled his lordship's body up in the Turkey carpet. Fortunately he was a small man, and I was able to carry him to the graveyard without too much difficulty. It was not overly burdensome to loosen the soil in the rector's grave, and I placed his lordship's body in the ground on top of the coffin and filled the hole with soil once more before saying a prayer for the dead, as I am most punctilious in these matters and can always be relied upon to fulfil such little tasks as often fall to the hand of a willing clergyman.

Then I returned to the house. Of course, I did not expect to see her ladyship, as it was now five and thirty in the morning and the sun was only just starting to rise. I returned to my room to make my ablutions with the pitcher of cold water that had been thoughtfully provided the previous night, and was pleasantly surprised to see a set of clergyman's clothes upon my bed. From their size, I supposed them to have been left by Mr. Stephens, though how her ladyship found them (for indeed, it must have been she who supplied them) I cannot say. After washing myself, I managed to struggle into them (Mr. Stephens having a shorter, leaner body than my own) and later made my way to the breakfast-room.

I had not supposed her ladyship would be present for breakfast, but she was already at table.

'There you are,' she said, in a voice that some would have thought disapproving. 'It does not do to be late for breakfast. I hope nothing has happened to detain you?'

I was somewhat astonished that she seemed already to have forgotten the events of the night, but I know that such matters may be too distressing for the gentle sex to contemplate, and I felt she was entirely justified in not dwelling on such an unpleasant episode. And of course, she could not have mentioned it in the presence of her servants.

At the end of breakfast, she nodded at me and said, 'I am afraid Sir Lewis was unable to be present. He was called on very suddenly to depart for France, and I fear the state of battle there gives little hope he will ever return. This means, of course, that I will eventually inherit his estate. I would be grateful, therefore, if you would accept the living here. There is a cottage on the edge of my grounds, and the position will be yours as long as I see fit. I am sure I can rely upon your discretion.' And she raised her left eyebrow slightly.

'Of course, your ladyship,' I replied, overcome with gratitude at such graciousness.

And that, my dear Anne, is how I came to take on the living of Rosings Park, under the most bountiful patronage of your mother, Lady Catherine de Bourgh.

Chapter 3

Mrs. Bennet – The Venus of Pemberley

Well, my dear sister, I thank you for undertaking to write these events down for me and to pass the story on once I am gone, which will not be long, I'm sure, given the state of my nerves. I know my family will understand my motives for what took place, and will forgive me for the little liberty I was forced to take.

You will recall the wedding of my eldest daughter, Jane. Such a beauty, and the event was widely talked of in the village. Never such a fine-looking bride. And Bingley such a wealthy husband. And so good-natured. And my second daughter, Lizzy, although she had not such good looks as Jane, she did very well for herself. I dare say she schemed and plotted in secret for some time with Mr. Bennet, for she could not have secured such a husband as Mr. Darcy had it not been for the help of her father. But would they tell me? Not a bit of it. But there. She made a good match and we were grateful. Though such a hard, arrogant man as she had chosen. I shall never forget how he snubbed me at Netherfield. When they announced their engagement, I will admit I was lost for words, but the more I thought about it, the more I remembered how he had slighted us. I had a good mind not to visit them, but poor dear Lydia was in Newcastle with Wickham and prevailed on me to take a trip to the North with Mr. and Mrs. Gardiner, and as my travelling companions would go by way of Pemberley, I had no choice but to go with them, though it was most vexatious to my poor nerves.

The journey there was frightful. I thought we should never get away from Longbourn, what with the fuss about the Gardiners' children, and their mother assuring them they would be well looked after by Mary and Kitty. And then we could not find Kitty anywhere and she had to be fetched from Meryton, where she was paying a visit to Maria Lucas. And when she did return we could not find Mary, because *she* was in the church playing on Mr. Collins's organ and did not wish to be interrupted. And what with one thing and another, our journey north was much delayed. And Mrs. Gardiner would not allow me to take all my valises and parcels, as she said they would be too weighty for the horses, and I had to leave behind many of the presents I had bought for poor Lydia, besides the crewel work I had spent all winter preparing for her. It was most upsetting, and I dare say we should never have got away, had not Mr. Bennet prevailed on the Gardiners to make haste. Indeed, I was becoming quite distressed, and it was his kindness that enabled us to leave while the maid was still looking for my smelling salts. He was so happy to see us depart safely that he smiled more than I have seen him smile since Jane and Lizzy's wedding.

Well, we travelled for many hours and eventually reached Oxford. Such a grand place, with its famous university. We passed the night there in an hotel, and I wished Kitty had been with us, as there were a great many good-looking young men and she could have made a match with any one of them. Even Mary would have found some one suitable. I am sure there were enough parsons and curates in training to satisfy *her*.

But after Oxford the journey was quite tedious, with nothing but dismal countryside all around us, and some dreary villages. I cannot see why people praise towns like Warwick. There is nothing there except an old castle. And as for Birmingham—it is a very dull place indeed, with very little charm. I suppose the Royal Hotel is well enough, with its chandeliers and mirrors, but we were not there in the season and there was little to recommend the town itself. There are streets full of workshops and shopfronts full of buttons, besides a number of pawn shops for the numerous poverty-stricken residents. It is a much poorer sort of place than Meryton, with a lesser class of person. I bought some sets of pearl buttons for Lydia. Mr. Gardiner bought a telescopic toasting-fork and teased us endlessly with it on the next stage of the journey. I could quite have throttled him.

Eventually we reached Pemberley. Lizzy was waiting at the main entrance and was overjoyed to see us. Mrs. Gardiner also was effusive in her greeting, and took so much charge of the situation that Lizzy barely had time to talk to me. But she was always her *father's* favourite.

I dare say the approach to Pemberley is quite grand, but for myself I think it is very ostentatious. People with money should be more circumspect in displaying their wealth. It is courting trouble to have such an imposing approach to so vast a house—an open invitation to thieves and lower sorts of people. And as for the interior, one would think the opposite would be true—a chance to demonstrate their fortune with a show of jewelled ornaments and expensive paintings. But no, not a bit of it. I suppose some might call the furniture elegant, but it is too plain for my taste. And the numerous windows that make the house so bright. They take no account of the sun, which is ruining the curtains, and indeed, Lizzy's skin was unbecomingly brown. But there. *She* had no need to worry, now she had snared a rich husband. And the colour of the wall paint—celestial blue, Mrs. Gardiner called it. I thought it a rather subdued shade of green. Very dull indeed.

Now, if they had asked me how to furnish and decorate the house, I could have recommended more brightly patterned wallpaper, with gold tassels for all the curtains. But I saved those ideas for Lydia. I knew she would agree with me on the need for gaiety. I will allow that the India paper on my bedroom wall looked well enough, and the ceiling rose was pleasant to look at, I suppose. But how I craved my apartment at Longbourn, with its gilded furniture and rich ruby brocade curtains, and our splendid chandelier.

The fact is, Mr. Bennet's two thousand a year were not enough to keep us in the latest fashions. I was badly let down. My own father left me four thousand pounds, but of course I had no knowledge of these things and I thought that meant four thousand a year; but no, it was all I had in the world to live on, and with Mr. Bennet's house entailed, it would go very badly for us when he passed. I suppose he was trying to economise, but it meant our house was very dull and would scarcely attract the kind of young men to keep Mary and Kitty in comfort. But there. If my husband died, the girls and I must go and live with Mr. Bingley and Jane. *She* would look after us. Darcy and Lizzy would be far too proud to welcome her poor relations. But what if Jane did not want us after all? I cannot say I felt very welcome when we visited her. I even overheard Bingley whisper to Jane on one occasion that they should hint at my departure. She rebuked him, but not without a gentle sigh that seemed to indicate agreement.

Thoughts of our future thus plagued me constantly, and I longed to have some independent means of providing for myself and my unmarried daughters. Something of value, perhaps, that I could sell if our circumstances became reduced. It was this that led me to examine the furnishings around me more carefully after dinner. Lizzy and the Gardiners were playing on the pianoforte in the drawing-room, and the music was so loud it set my nerves jangling, and so I went for a little walk. On a high up ledge in a room in one of the far-flung guest suites was a small bronze statuette, less than a foot high. It shewed a naked woman with a cloth draped over her left thigh, her left foot resting on a small platform. Some Venus, I supposed. Her curly hair was piled on her head and she was washing herself with a little kerchief in her left hand. Her figure was very pleasing, much as my own was, I must admit, before the carriage of five daughters quite ravaged my body. High in a corner of the same room was another bronze statue, less than six inches tall, of a peasant in a large hat, with a bag and a coat over his shoulders. Trinkets to one such as Mr. Darcy. His house was full of such things. Indeed, it seemed a waste to have such ornaments when there was no one to regard them. They would be worth a mere trifle to him. Why should they not be borrowed by some one less fortunate than himself?

The next day, I waited until the others were gone to take a turn about the garden. My nerves were torn to shreds after our long coach journey, and so I stayed in the breakfast-room. Once the rest of the party were gone outside, however, I made my way to the furthest wing of the house and entered the apartment with the statuettes. The shelves were too high for me to reach, but I pushed a little chair up to the corner and was endeavouring to put my hand on the bronze peasant when I was disturbed by a sound from without and heard a maid clattering up the staircase with some cleaning implements. I immediately replaced the chair, and, not wanting to be found alone in the unoccupied guest suite, I stepped behind the yellow velvet curtain that fell from the ceiling to the floor in front of the double window.

No sooner had I hid, than the maid entered the room and made a cursory attempt to dust the tables and sweep the carpets. I suppose there was not much to do, since the suite was unused, but I thought she was making a very poor fist of it. Mr. Darcy should have been much more careful whom he chose to employ. I would have told him myself, had it not been necessary to conceal my observations. She was there no more than five minutes before she left the room, and I heard her disappearing down the staircase. I waited to make sure she was quite gone before I too went along the corridor and descended the stairs.

The rest of the party were now assembled in the drawing-room, and we spent the remainder of the day visiting the estate. The men did a little fishing and the ladies walked around the grounds, Lizzy and Mrs. Gardiner taking an inordinate interest in the plants and cuttings. I suppose that is all very well for women who have nothing better to do. Goodness knows, I had more valuable calls on my time at Longbourn.

The evening was similarly trying. Darcy prevailed on Lizzy to play on the pianoforte again and sing a duet with him. She has not half Mary's talent, and I ventured to suggest that Mary accompany us on our next visit, so they could hear how the pianoforte might be used to real advantage in such a setting. Mr. Darcy smiled at Lizzy and said she had delighted us all long enough and should allow another young lady to play next time, and they both laughed heartily, which I must say was very bewildering. We had a little night-cap and repaired to bed, not before time. My head was aching from the noise of the pianoforte and the unrelenting sun in the garden.

The next morning, I found Mr. Gardiner in the break-fast-room demonstrating his toasting-fork at the hearth. It was a most undignified display of merriment as he toasted several pieces of bread, dropping some in the fire and burning the others. Mrs. Gardiner ate one with butter and pronounced it delicious, but they could not persuade me to try one. However, it did give me an idea. I waited until the gentlemen were gone fishing in the lake, Mr. Darcy having prevailed upon Mr. Gardiner to accompany him again. Lizzy and Mrs. Gardiner went out to the plant nursery. I felt slighted that they did not urge me to go with them, but it gave me an opportunity to retrieve the discarded toasting-fork and make my way to the unoccupied guest suite.

Once there, I again pulled the chair up to the shelf and, extending the toasting-fork, I was able to knock the little bronze peasant statue to the floor. It fell with a gentle thud onto the carpet, and I immediately placed it in my workbag. Then I moved the chair to beneath the other ledge and was about to perform the same manoeuvre with the fork when I heard voices in the corridor. This time it was the maid and a groom. They were laughing as they approached the room, and I just had time to hide behind the curtain.

'I think you need to dust more carefully, miss,' says the groom.

'Come here, then, and inspect my work more closely,' says the maid.

I could see nothing through the curtain, but needed not to have borne five children to know they were well on their way to starting their own family there on the guest bed. It was all very well, but they were being paid to work, not to disport themselves in this fashion.

I thought they should never be done, but eventually a bell rang and I could hear them hastily pulling on their clothes and scurrying down the corridor. I quickly gained access to the Venus statuette and added it to my workbag before returning quietly to my own bedroom. Then I returned the toasting-fork to the breakfast-room and drank a cup of tea. My nerves were all a-jingle.

The rest of the day, and, indeed, the following week, passed much as the first day had done. We made some excursions into the surrounding country-side and saw some pretty views, though nothing to compare with Longbourn. And finally we were ready to leave for Newcastle.

On the last morning, the servants were gathered to farewell us on the steps to the main house, and there I almost met with disaster. The maid was helping the groom attach our belongings to the coach, when a most unfortunate accident occurred. My trunk containing the bronze statuettes fell to the ground, dislodging the lid. The bronze peasant remained hid in my night-dress in the bottom of the trunk, but the Venus rolled onto the grass. The maid was quick to seize it, and she and the groom looked at me in wonderment. No one else had noticed, their attention being drawn to a servant who was passing Mr. Gardiner his toasting-fork, amid much merriment.

'Upon my word,' I said, 'I do not know how that statue came to be in my trunk. I wonder who can have put it there? I am sure it was a mistake. Perhaps you could replace it in the guest room when you are cleaning there—you and the groom. Together.' And I gave them a very meaningful look. She coloured, and he turned redder than Kitty does when caught eating fruit in the strawberry patch.

'Of course, madam,' she said, and concealed the statue in her apron.

'Come, come,' said Mr. Gardiner. 'It is time to depart.'

And so we climbed into the carriage. Mr. Darcy and Lizzy took their farewells, the servants bowed and waved, and the maid and the groom stood at the back and nodded slowly to me. I could see that my quick thinking had averted a catastrophe, and although I had lost the Venus, the borrowed peasant would see me and my girls through several years of hardship, should the need arise.

For I do not care what any one says; it is hard to be a woman when one's husband's estate is entailed.

CHAPTER 4

MARY BENNET – THE DEVIL'S INTERVAL

I am, as my father has been used to acknowledge, a deeply reflective young lady; and, as my mother concedes, my musical taste and talent are excellent, so that I am regarded as being more accomplished than any one in our neighbourhood. It is for this reason I devote so much time to improving my performance upon the pianoforte and the church organ. There are only two of us at home now with my parents. I am sure it would be beneficial to my art, were I to attend a music conservatorium to advance my studies, and I am sorry I did not attempt to go to Cambridge and join in my sister Lizzy's procession in support of women's education. But it behoves me to maintain the tone of our family and promote us in a good light before the village, for what is the point of girlhood, but to improve each shining hour? There are some who have tried to interrupt my musical renditions, but I will not foreshorten a piece or omit the repeat sections merely to enhance the listener's enjoyment.

For this reason, I spend much time in the church practising on the organ. It is a magnificent instrument, bestowed on us by Mr. Collins as a token of his good will when he became the rector at Rosings. Lady Catherine had complained that the church there needed a newer instrument, such as the one we were favoured with here at St. Jude's, and she recommended that the old Rosings organ be donated in exchange. Mr. Collins's kindness in arranging the transfer was largely unacknowledged by the villagers in Longbourn, and indeed, the regular organist, Mr. Stoppe, was in high dudgeon, claiming that our new instrument was inferior and 'too full of wind, like its donor'.

I am sure I do not know what Mr. Stoppe was complaining about, as the Rosings organ is perfectly adequate for our little church, and has the added distinction of having previously graced a building of great importance. I therefore endeavour to practise my pieces in the church every day, and it was on one such occasion, when I was immersed in Bach's Toccata and Fugue in D minor, that I had the great good fortune, as I then thought, to encounter Mr. Collins himself. I had heard that he and his wife Charlotte were visiting her parents at Lucas Lodge, and I had observed them all at church on Sunday morning. It was an even greater excitement to me when Mr. Collins preached the sermon. He seemed such an eloquent fellow, and talked such a deal of sense. Indeed, I did not know why my sister Kitty was giggling and Maria Lucas rolling her eyes. I thought if they had paid attention to the teaching instead of commenting on their friends' bonnets and stroking their own vanity, they would have been amply repaid for their solicitude. I had hoped to have the honour to play the organ myself during that service, but the vicar would not allow it. I suppose Mr. Stoppe plays every week, but that is all the more reason to allow other musicians to take a turn.

I therefore returned to the church that afternoon and was soon buried in my favourite piece. It was a fitting accompaniment to the inclement, nay, wild weather, with thunder rolling around the roof, and lightning fit to strike the steeple. Imagine my amazement, therefore, when I heard the church door creak, and saw Mr. Collins enter and take a pew near the organ seat. (For St. Jude's is quite small and we do not have an organ loft.) He was wet through, and his hat, which he placed on the pew next to him, was dripping with rain.

'Pray do not allow me to intrude,' he said, and I continued my playing.

It is a very powerful piece of music and I have spent much time analysing it. Mr. Collins listened to the end, with only a few interruptions, as when he started to clap each time I paused at a rest.

'That is a very enjoyable piece,' he said. 'Of course, I do not understand music, but if I may be permitted to say, I think some of your notes may be a little inaccurate. It may be the composer made a mistake, or perhaps the instrument needs tuning. I would not like to say you played a false note.'

I was somewhat mystified, but then I realised he was talking about the tritones. I played that part of the fugue again.

'Are these the notes?' I asked.

'The very same,' he replied.

'In that case,' I said, 'there is no mistake. Those are tritones. Augmented fourths. They have an unusual kind of interval between the notes, where three whole tones are played together. It produces an uncommon effect in the listener.'

He looked at me a little oddly.

'Yes,' he said. 'Indeed it does.'

He said no more about the piece, but offered to walk me home to Longbourn. The storm had abated, and we had a most agreeable conversation on the way. I thought him such a wise man, most appreciative of my own intelligence. At the door, he said we must meet again and continue his musical instruction. Then he left me, as he wanted to talk to my parents, but my mother had just departed to Pemberley with my uncle and aunt, and though I was sure I had seen a curtain move in my father's library as we approached the house, he was nowhere to be seen. Mr. Collins therefore bade me adieu and insinuated he would be delighted to see me again at St. Jude's.

I was in a fever of anticipation all night, for it was not every day, thought I, that a young lady was invited to display her talents to so distinguished an audience.

The next day, I endeavoured to get away early, but was much delayed by my young Gardiner cousins, who were staying with us while my uncle and aunt were at Pemberley. They demanded to be entertained in the garden, and would keep bowling hoops and throwing balls to me till I was quite exhausted. After tea, I told Kitty it was her turn to look after them. Then I put on my new brown muslin and hastened to the church.

To my great pleasure, Mr. Collins was strolling outside the building, admiring the gravestones and trudging up and down on the most recent burial sites. He explained he was testing the firmness of the soil after the rain.

'For,' said he, 'we would not want any of the ladies to be inconvenienced by loose stones and mud when they are making their way in to the service.'

I considered this very thoughtful of him. He appeared so solicitous of other people's feelings and so anxious to please the gentler sex. And I must admit, his company was indeed agreeable. At least, I found it so. Kitty could go hang. What did she know of the behaviour of a true gentleman?

'Let us go into the church,' he said, 'for I am desirous of hearing your music again.'

He took my arm and we entered the vestibule together, my heart pounding wildly in my breast, so that I thought he should have heard it, but he made no remark and sat himself down in the pew nearest the organ stool. I seated myself at the keyboard and played again for him Bach's Toccata and Fugue.

At the end, his face was quite red. He clapped his hands, but shook his head. 'Are you sure you are not mistaken?' he asked. 'Tell me again, what are those notes that sound strangely?'

'Tritones, sir,' I answered.

'Indeed,' he said, 'now I have time to consider them, I find them most stimulating.'

His speech was broken up by a sudden shortness of breath, and he whipped his hat off his head and held it in front of him.

'It is very warm in here,' he said, fanning his face with his free hand.

'Indeed it is,' I replied. 'Let me take your hat.'

I reached forward to take his headpiece, but he sprang back, all the while holding the hat in front of him, close to his person.

'No, no,' he cried. 'I will keep it. Let me escort you to your house.'

We walked home in a most peculiar manner, my right hand tucked into his left arm, his right hand firmly clenching the hat before him, as though it were glued to the top of his legs. The afternoon was no longer warm, and there was a cold breeze riffling the ends of his hair, but he would not don the hat, despite my attempts to persuade him.

'Thank you for a most . . . invigorating afternoon,' he said. Then he handed me a book wrapped in brown paper, and bowed solemnly before walking away. I watched him from the window, and as soon as he had quitted the garden, he put his hat back on his head and walked on in a spritely manner.

It was time for dinner when I entered the house, so I hid the book behind some others on Lydia's bookshelf, to open later, knowing that her apartment was undisturbed since her departure.

During our evening meal, I was still musing on my meeting with Mr. Collins, though I was interrupted many times by Kitty.

'What do you suppose my sister Lydia is doing now?' said she.

Our father looked heavenwards, then frowned and addressed Kitty. 'Your sister Lydia is a foolish young woman, and is not worthy of further thought until she has learned to control her actions. Is that not so, Mary?'

I was pleased that he considered my opinion worth consulting, for I pride myself on the solidity of my judgments. 'Quite so,' I said. 'For, as I told Elizabeth at the time of Lydia's great disgrace, we cannot be too guarded in our conduct towards the less worthy of the other sex.'

Kitty choked on her mutton. 'Are you sure you are entirely guarded in your conduct towards that oaf Mr. Collins?'

'Mr. Collins?' said our father. 'What has he to do with the matter?'

'Mary is playing with his organ,' said Kitty. And she gave me a defiant look.

My father turned to me, but I had nothing to hide.

'It is true,' I declared. 'I practise every day in church. For some one in this family must be musical, Kitty. We cannot all spend our time dressing bonnets and flirting with officers.'

'Flirting with officers?' asked our father. 'Kitty, what is this? I had thought there were no officers now in Longbourn.'

'They are nearly all gone, sir,' she said, and poked her tongue at me when he turned to carve the meat.

'And stop sticking your tongue out at your sister,' he added. 'The sooner you can go back to Jane and Bingley's house, the better. I had thought you were of a less impressionable frame after so much time in their company, but it seems there is room for further improvement. Is that not so, Mary?'

'Indeed it is,' I replied. And I must confess, I put my own tongue out at Kitty when my father was not watching.

After dinner, I hastened to Lydia's chamber and found the volume Mr. Collins had given me. Then I slipped into my own room, closed the door and opened the book with trembling fingers. It was by a man named Mr. Cleland, and the story, *Fanny Hill, or Memoirs of a Woman of Pleasure*, was engrossing. Indeed, I could not put it down, and I read and read all night until I had finished it. I understood Mr.

Collins was trying to communicate a message to me through this book, and I was all anticipation of our next meeting.

I went to St. Jude's directly after breakfast, and I played all morning on the organ, but Mr. Collins did not come. When I returned home, I was heartily disappointed to learn he had departed for Rosings, but I resolved to improve my performance, the better to impress him on his return. I also passed much time in reflection on his hat. Now I had read the book, I had a clearer idea of what he was trying to conceal.

The book greatly inflamed me, and I was exceedingly envious of Mr. Collins's wife, Charlotte. It was a great trial to me to see her nearly every day, as she had stayed on to visit her parents, and frequently accompanied her sister Maria on her calls to my sister Kitty. It was on one such visit that I had a very great idea. Charlotte provoked me constantly, even more so because she was heedless of what I then deemed to be Mr. Collins's extreme worthiness, and would say only that they spent a great deal of time apart and that she found the trial of separation one which she could easily bear. I thought she was not a fit match for such an estimable character as her husband, and I resolved to redress the situation should the opportunity arise.

It was only a few days before such an occasion presented itself. Kitty and I had taken the Gardiner children to the river for a picnic, and Maria and Charlotte joined us there with their younger brothers and sisters. The river was shallow at this spot, but it became deeper further along, and I warned the children not to get their feet wet. As soon as we reached the place, however, the elder ones tore their shoes and socks off and waded in, while the younger children paddled in the shallows. They made a great deal of noise as they splashed each other, and I was obliged to move away from the bank, as my dress was quite wet. Kitty and Maria set out a picnic blanket and a cold collation for our refreshment, while Charlotte watched the children from the water's edge at the point where the river became deeper. I joined her, thinking to engage in conversation.

'How you must miss your husband,' said I. 'I do not think I could endure a separation such as yours.'

'I find I can bear it very well,' she replied.

'And yet, he has given us such a fine organ,' I said.

She looked at me strangely for a moment, and then said, 'You mean the instrument in your church? Yes, indeed, the old organ from Rosings is . . . of great value, now Lady Catherine no longer has need of it.'

'Do you not enjoy playing with Mr. Collins's organ?' I asked, leading her closer to the river.

'I do not,' said she. 'I have never been musical, and I am afraid the organ in the church at Rosings is quite wasted on me.'

'That is a pity,' I said, taking her by the elbow. 'But perhaps you prefer the consolations of nature? This river, for example, is very pretty, is it not?'

'Indeed it is,' said she.

'And look,' I said. 'There is a kingfisher!'

I reached out over the water, my hand still on her arm, and she leaned out with me. Then all of a sudden, I am sure I do not know how, she tripped, and toppled into the water. It was very deep and she was unable to swim. Several times she went under, and the current was starting to drag her down the stream. I knew not what to do. Then I heard a shout of alarm. It was Edward, Charlotte's younger brother.

'Charlotte!' he cried. 'Catch hold of that branch.'

There was a long branch from a sycamore tree stretching into the middle of the river where Charlotte was being carried by the current. She held it fast with both hands and was able to check her progress. Edward was a good swimmer, and he had no difficulty reaching her and helping her to safety. On the bank, she stood shivering and trembling, and thanking Edward profusely.

'For without you,' she said, 'I am sure I should have been drowned.'

Kitty and Maria made much of her, and wrapped the picnic blanket around her. We abandoned our excursion and made our way back to Lucas Lodge, the children excited by their adventure and we girls going over and over again the accident that had befallen Charlotte.

'What happened?' asked Kitty.

'She slipped,' I said.

Charlotte gave me a look that was partly pity and partly disbelief. 'I do not want to think ill of you, Mary, but I do believe you pushed me.'

'I?' I exclaimed. 'My dear Charlotte. You are quite mistaken.'

'I do not think so,' she said. 'You were holding my elbow and pulling me out over the water, and then, all of a sudden, you pushed me hard and I fell.'

'Oh, my dear Charlotte,' I said again, beside myself that my little plan should be so quickly uncovered. 'How ever can you say such a thing? I am only sorry I could not rescue you myself, but I cannot swim.'

'But neither did you call for help,' she said in an accusing tone.

'It is true,' I replied, after some reflection. 'I was so stunned by the accident that my voice quite dried up and I was unable to move or speak. Is it not fortunate that the young ones have no such impediments? Your brother Edward is quite the hero, is he not?'

'Yes,' said she, moving away from me and taking Maria's arm. 'I suppose he is.'

'Indeed,' said Kitty. 'What a tale we shall have to tell my Aunt Gardiner when she returns.'

Charlotte remained at Lucas Lodge for several weeks and refused to visit our house, and though she initially took a cold, she was soon recovered and ready to return to Rosings. I, for my part, did not wish to see her ever again.

Mr. Collins did not hasten to return after her accident, as Lady Catherine had other duties for him to perform, but by and bye he arranged to come and convey Charlotte home in the post-chaise. I was in a fever of anticipation, for had not Mr. Collins given me the book that was now my nightly companion, and would he not wish to engage in some happy intercourse on it with me?

The morning before their departure, Mr. Collins graced me again with his company at St. Jude's. The day was blustery, and I was deep in my private performance of Bach's Toccata and Fugue when I felt a great gust of wind, which swirled the dried leaves into the church and along the nave, and there before me was Mr. Collins. He doffed his hat and smiled graciously, and I stopped my playing to greet him.

'Mr. Collins. I am very pleased to see you. I would like to thank you . . .'

'And I am pleased to see you.' He beamed. 'I have something of substance to impart. I have been doing my own researches, and her ladyship has most kindly allowed her church organist to instruct me in musical theory. I have discovered, Mary,' and here his voice took on a graver tone, 'that this music you are playing is sinful. Nay, more, it is of the devil.'

I raised my head in consternation. 'I am very sorry, sir, but I believe Bach is a great musician and would not knowingly write any thing diabolical. What is wrong with this piece?'

'Pray, play it again.'

I commenced from the beginning, and after several bars he stopped me.

'There. That is it. The *diabolus in musica*.'

'Do you mean the tritones?' I asked.

He shook his head. 'I do not remember the musical term, but I know the sound. It is most unsettling.' And he started to play nervously with his hat, placing it on his lap and moving the brim in circles with his fingertips.

I played the bars again.

He closed his eyes and grimaced. 'It is the devil's interval,' he whispered.

Now I felt somewhat indignant. I had practised this piece very often, and though my estimation of Mr. Collins was great, my respect for Mr. Bach's music was even greater. What is more, this was my favourite piece. When I played it, I felt relieved of my earthly burdens and able to reach my true self, the self I endeavoured to hide from my sisters. For, though Lydia and Kitty were used to behave with intemperance and flirtation, I knew that young ladies were supposed to act with circumspection and modesty, like Jane and Lizzy. And was not this piece a hidden doorway to the darker regions of my soul, furnishing me with secret gratification while I yet maintained a respectable demeanour? It did not seem fair that three of my sisters were married, and Kitty had her soldiers, but I, who tried always to do what was right, was left quite alone. Books and music were my only solace, and Mr. Collins was trying to put a stop to my innocent musical pleasure.

And so I decided to take matters into my own hands. I played again the Toccata and Fugue, the notes tripping over each other in their haste, the music's grand awfulness swelling to fill the church with its majesty, while Mr. Collins stayed in his pew, transported, his face the colour of stripped rhubarb. And when I had finished, I marched out of the church with him, and at the very last I seized his hat, which he was again holding in front of him below his waist.

Mr. Collins turned even redder in the face and snatched the hat from my grasp.

'I am afraid I must take my leave,' he said, 'for we are departing very soon. My wife . . . I do not wish to be late . . . Lady Catherine . . .'

He hastened away, and I was obliged to walk home on my own.

Now I no longer wanted his book. I did not wish to keep it in my room, and so I thought to return it to Lydia's. It was the sort of book which she would enjoy, thought I, and she would not know whence it had come. So I wrapped it again in brown paper and slid it behind the other books on her shelves, and as I did so, another volume fell to the ground. It too was covered in brown paper. I picked it up and saw it was addressed to me, so I tore off the covering. It was a copy of Fordyce's *Sermons to Young Women*, and on the inside cover was an inscription to me from Mr. Collins. I returned to my room with it and proceeded to rip the pages to shreds.

Later that night, I reflected. It is true I was disappointed by my discovery about the book. But I took some comfort in what I had seen when I snatched Mr. Collins's hat. The bulge that it concealed was pitifully small—and I no longer envied Charlotte Lucas.

Chapter 5

Mr. Darcy – A Burning Desire

I ran as fast as I could, red-faced and breathless, until I reached the grounds of Pemberley. Then I stripped to my undergarments and plunged into the lake, letting the sparkling clear water cool my body until I emerged clean and fresh. I drew my white muslin shirt on over my head and donned my waistcoat, tugged my short drawers over the top of my breeches, and made my way towards the house, my shirt clinging to my wet chest.

After our marriage, Elizabeth and I lived quietly at Pemberley, and were able, by various stratagems, to forestall too frequent visits from my in-laws. Elizabeth missed her father, but she was more than happy to shorten her mother's visits, and Jane and Bingley, for all their long-suffering virtue, did not encourage Mrs. Bennet to prolong her stays with them. We saw the Bingleys frequently, as they had removed to an estate in the neighbouring county, but Mr. and Mrs. Hurst were more often in London, and Bingley's sister Caroline was much occupied elsewhere, for which I was relieved. My sister Georgiana continued with us, and she and Lizzy became the firmest of friends.

At breakfast on one of their visits, Bingley was reading from the newspaper, and was much struck by an article of local interest.

'What do you make of this, Darcy?' said he. ' "Masked criminal on the run. A masked felon was seen setting fire to the barn of Mr. John Winterbottom, of the parish of Lambton, on Sunday last. The fire was extinguished, but not before a number of kegs of beer had been destroyed. There was no damage to persons on the scene. This is the second event of this type in this area, after Mr. Higginbottom's hay cart was burned last year." '

'How very troubling,' said Jane. 'I wonder what could have caused the criminal to act in this way? Surely no one could commit such a felony without being severely provoked?'

My dear sister-in-law is ever looking for explanations for villainous behaviour, and ascribing innocent motives to the most shocking of offenders.

'Were you not a friend of Mr. Winterbottom as a child, my dear?' asked Elizabeth.

'Indeed he was,' said Bingley. 'Surely you remember him, Darcy? Upon my soul, I do not like to speak ill of any one, but I remember he treated you appallingly badly. Did he not set fire to your wooden boats?'

'He may have done,' I answered. 'I do not recall. We were very young.'

It was not an incident I wished to dwell upon.

'Then I think he fully deserves the loss of his kegs of beer,' said Bingley. 'I hope it may teach him a lesson.'

'Let us hope so,' I said.

Then I turned the subject to fishing, and no more was said.

I was walking with Elizabeth and Georgiana in the grounds a few weeks later when we came upon our housekeeper, Mrs. Reynolds, and her grandson. They were in the kitchen garden, helping one of the maids pick carrots, and the little fellow was very disconsolate. When I asked what the trouble was, Mrs. Reynolds was indignant.

'It's that Thomas Longbottom,' she said. 'He was playing with little William here, and he asked to borrow William's hobby-horse, the one his late aunt gave him. It's a toy horse on a stick, and it's got a mane and a bridle, and it looks very smart, doesn't it, William?'

William only nodded. I could see he was trying to restrain his tears.

'Well, William gives him the horse, and then this Thomas snaps the pole in two and rips the hair out and throws the horse in the lake. And then he laughs at William and calls him a baby. And William's only three, sir, but he's as bold as any.'

William nodded. I could see he was trying not to cry, but the tears welled up from his big brown eyes and his fat little cheeks were red with misery.

'My auntie made it,' he said. 'My auntie what's died. And she can't ever make another.'

Mrs. Reynolds gathered him in her arms. 'There there, my pet. I will make you another horse, and your auntie will look down on you from heaven and be happy. Come, now, and help pull these carrots.'

Elizabeth and I walked on with Georgiana, and when I put my arm round my wife's waist I could feel her heart beating with indignation.

'Do you know this Longbottom family, dearest?' she asked me.

'Indeed I do,' I said. 'They are a most unpleasant household, well known in this neighbourhood.'

'Then no one would be offended if their shed were to burn down,' she said, her merry eyes twinkling with mischief.

'My dear,' I said, 'you know that the penalty for arson is transportation at the least, or hanging at the worst. Surely people like the Longbottoms are not worth a punishment such as that?'

'You are right,' she said. 'But a penalty is only meted out to some one who is caught. You know, my dearest, that I have a great desire for justice to be done.'

I knew Lizzy was more courageous than almost any one else of my acquaintance, and had braved the law-courts in support of women's education. She had lately taken to mysterious meetings and night-time excursions of which I was not always permitted to know the details, so I warned her again of the seriousness of a crime such as arson. She would only laugh and say that justice was justice, and some one who was foolish enough to be caught was not a suitable person to exact retribution on others. Georgiana looked on in silence, but I noticed that she and Elizabeth exchanged secretive glances when they thought I was not looking.

It was Mrs. Reynolds who informed us the following week of how Thomas Longbottom's mother and father had wakened all their neighbours in the middle of the night with their appalling shrieks. The parents had retired to bed, but in the small hours, Mrs. Longbottom put her hand out to push her husband, who was snoring loudly, and instead of Mr. Longbottom's chin, she encountered what she supposed to be the head of a dead horse. She screamed and screamed, but when her husband lit a candle, all they found was a toy. It was the size of a real horse's head, with glass eyes and a long mane, and in the dark it looked 'just like a real 'un', they claimed. The story was the talk of Lambton, and every time they walked down the street or into a shop, some one would be sure to whinny, or offer them a bag of oats, or try and stroke their hair. It was a most delightful outcome, and Mrs. Reynolds was all smiles when she narrated it to us.

'Do they have no idea who did this?' asked Elizabeth.

'No,' said Mrs. Reynolds. 'But after the fire and this horse, folk are on their guard.'

'I wonder,' said Elizabeth to me privately, 'if there is a pattern to all this? Winterbottom . . . Longbottom . . . Higginbottom . . . Surely it is unusual that all the victims have such similar surnames?'

'There are unfortunately several people known for their *base* behaviour in these parts,' I replied. I would not risk humour such as this with any one else, but my dear Lizzy understands me completely and appreciates my little jokes, as I appreciate hers. I truly never thought such felicity would be possible, but I am the happiest of men.

It was not always so. When I was a child, I was bullied unmercifully by the boys in the town. I was fastidious in my movements, preferring to approach things in a certain way. At meal-times, for instance, I had to sort the food on my plate into different sizes and eat the smallest pieces first, progressing to the largest. Any deviation from this routine would trouble me greatly. The other boys learned about this and called me a foozler and a gump, though I was neither clumsy nor foolish, and on one occasion, as Bingley rightly remembered, young John Winterbottom burned my entire wooden boat collection. I had been amassing the little vessels for several years. Some were given to me by my grandparents; others were made by our gardener; one I made myself, with much painstaking effort. I thought allowing the other boys to sail my collection on the lake would demonstrate my generosity of spirit and lead them to become my friends, but they capsized the boats, then fished them out of the water and built a bonfire.

'Look here,' said John Winterbottom. 'This'll dry your boats, Darcy.' And he set fire to the leaves and sticks and threw the boats on top, where they were slowly engulfed in flames. The other boys restrained me while they added fuel to the fire, and I was unable to stop them.

After this, the Bottom boys, as they were known, due to the unlikely coincidence of their surnames, gained a reputation for bullying behaviour, and I became known as a shy, unfriendly child, ill at ease in the presence of strangers, and best avoided by those who sought popularity. I was reluctant to tell my father, who wanted to believe only the best of people. My mother, a woman of firm and unwavering opinions, like her sister Lady Catherine, was hardly sympathetic. She offered to have the boys punished, and when I demurred, she washed her hands of the whole business and said I would face more serious trials when I was a man, and it was therefore high time I learned to take care of myself.

I did not forget the lads' behaviour, but as I grew older and inherited the estate, the tenants united in giving me a good name, and I merited a kind of grudging respect from the Bottom boys. This did not change my basic wariness of human interaction. I had no talent to converse with strangers, or to understand the true tone of a conversation. Happily, I am learning these skills from my dear Lizzy, and endeavouring to shew an interest in the concerns of others, though I draw the limit with my mother-in-law, as, indeed, does Mr. Bennet. I would invite the poor fellow to stay by himself and gain a little respite, but where he goes, his wife is sure to follow. I think he must lead a very dull life.

I have mentioned two of the Bottom boys—John Winterbottom and Thomas Longbottom. There were two more in the vicinity, to wit, Charles Higginbottom, whose hay stacks were burned, and Frederick Shufflebottom, as well as Frederick's two sisters, Sally and Susan. It was a veritable cornucopia of Bottoms for a small town, and may have been the result of earlier inbreeding, which might also account for the uncommonly high number of inhabitants with prominent jaws, large lower lips and hanging noses. Despite this, the parishioners are generally a kind and friendly group of people, and Elizabeth's Aunt Gardiner finds them quite charming.

'My dears,' said she, on one of her visits to Lambton, 'I read about the case of John Winterbottom in the newspaper. Is he quite recovered from the shock of the fire?'

Elizabeth looked at me. 'What say you, my dear? Is he recovered?'

'I imagine so,' I said.

'And the Longbottoms? I heard their name mentioned in the town.'

'Neigh,' I whinnied, 'I know not.'

Lizzy and Georgiana laughed so much at this that we were obliged to share the joke with the Gardiners, who were delighted.

'And are we to expect more vengeance on these people?' asked Mrs. Gardiner.

'Who knows?' said Elizabeth. 'Fitzwilliam told me long ago that once his good opinion was lost, it would never be regained.'

'Then there is a link between their treatment of Mr. Darcy and the retribution they are now experiencing?' asked Mr. Gardiner.

'I would not say that,' I said. 'Only that they will not easily regain *my* good opinion.'

'I am not surprised,' said Mrs. Gardiner. 'And I would not otherwise have mentioned it, but I heard a strange story yesterday at the inn in Lambton. Two young women and a young man were recounting an episode from their youth in which they said Mr. Wickham played a part. Wickham was only a boy, but he persuaded them to burn their friend's collection of toy boats. We dismissed it as childish memories, but now I am not so sure. Did you ever hear of such an episode?'

Georgiana turned pale. My dear Lizzy touched my hand and my sister's, and then poured us each a glass of Madeira. She looked at me, and I nodded.

'My dear aunt,' she said, 'you are not mistaken. Such an event did happen.' And she told them the whole story. 'But all that is long ago, and we are no longer offended, are we, my dear?'

I *was* no longer offended. But it was a strange coincidence that that very night, a haystack belonging to the Shufflebottom family was burned to the ground, the fire only being prevented from spreading by a stranger, who emptied a barrel of water on the flames before the alarm was raised, so that as the family came running to extinguish the fire, they found only the smouldering remains of their haystack and glimpsed in the distance a dark figure whose face was obscured by a mask.

Mrs. Reynolds informed us the next day that the townsfolk were in turmoil.

'It feels as though some one is seeking revenge, sir,' she said, 'but they do not know for what. Only, I heard some talk of your toy boats, and there were rumours that you have put some one up to it. I told them it was nonsense, but you should be careful, sir. Of course you're innocent, but Lord knows, it wants only for some one to put ideas into their heads. I am thankful there is no one who would play a trick like that.'

I was thankful too. I could take care of myself, but I did not want Elizabeth or Georgiana to be involved in such unpleasantness. Mrs. Reynolds was mistaken that no one would want to harm us, however, for only a week later, word reached me that Mr. Wickham was in the town. He had left his wife behind and come to see me in an attempt to extort funds. I had already settled more money on the scoundrel than I wanted, when he married Lydia, but he had soon run through that allowance, and now he had abandoned his commission, he was heavily in debt.

He first approached Lizzy, encountering her by chance when she went into the town with the Gardiners. She dismissed all his entreaties for a loan and bade him stay away from Pemberley. She related to me that evening that Lydia had frequently importuned her to ask me for money, but she had declined, instead providing a little out of her own income, though not nearly enough to meet all the Wickhams' profligate expenses. I was touched by her concern for my welfare, and had in any case always accorded her the dignity of doing as she would with her own money, without question. She said Wickham was very loath to part and had given her a most spiteful look, with a veiled threat that I should watch my sister and ensure she did not take part in any more unlicensed behaviour.

The thought of this scoundrel sullying my sister's name was more than I could bear. I enquired of Mrs. Reynolds where he was staying, and when I learned he was at the inn near Charles Higginbottom's farm, I determined to visit him on the morrow and have it out with him.

Before that, however, I wanted to visit the Higginbottoms and see for myself what might be done to ensure Wickham did not return to Lambton. I therefore dressed in a dark cloak and hat, shouldered a large sack of shavings from the woodshed, and set off on foot, as the quietest means of reaching the property without alerting suspicion. Once near the farmhouse, I could discern figures moving inside, illuminated by lamps and candles. I had a feeling of being watched, but there was no one in sight, and after waiting immobile for a good ten minutes, I felt I was safe and it was only my anxiety that conjured phantoms in the night. The season's hay was neatly stacked in a field, near enough to be seen from the house, but far enough not to pose any danger to life or limb. I scattered a bag of wood shavings near the largest haystack and proceeded to the edge of town, sprinkling shavings as I went, until I found Wickham's horse in the stables behind the inn. There were two saddlebags tossed carelessly on the straw by the horse, and I filled these bags with wood shavings. Then I returned to the haystack and took out my tinder box. I waited until there was a merry blaze before shouting, 'Fire!' Was it my imagination, or did a faint, repeated cry of 'Fire' echo my own?

I did not stop to find out, but ran as fast as I could, red-faced and breathless, until I reached the grounds of Pemberley, where I stripped to my undergarments and plunged into the lake. When I emerged, the ash was gone from my face and hair, and there was no trace of smoke. My body was wet and my shirt clung to my chest, so I wrapped my cloak around me and pulled my short drawers over my breeches for warmth. I did not expect to be seen at this hour of the night as I made my way to the house.

Despite my precautions, there was a light burning in Georgiana's chamber, and Lizzy was still awake when I reached our apartment.

'There you are, my dear,' she said. 'I have been waiting for you. Oh. You are wet!'

She looked me up and down, and a smile spread across her face. 'I do not know about the drawers on the outside of your breeches—I scarcely think they will be quite the thing at court—but that wet shirt is very becoming. Perhaps it is a fashion you should wear more often—when we are alone.'

She drew me to her and pulled the shirt over my head.

The next morning, Lizzy and Georgiana had the ponies harnessed and took the phaeton into the town, and I rode next to them on Phoenix, my magnificent bay stallion. We had anticipated a stroll along the main street, but the town was in an uproar, and the centre of the confusion was none other than George Wickham. He was surrounded by the Bottoms, led by Charles Higginbottom and his family. Higginbottom's nose was streaked with soot and his face was haggard.

'All night I fought that d*** fire,' he exclaimed. 'And this morning, what do I see? A pile of wood shavings. And where do they lead? Here, that's where!'

And he pointed dramatically to Wickham's saddlebags, just visible within the stable.

' 'Tis true,' echoed his neighbour Frederick. 'I seen 'em, an' all. There was a trail, wasn't there? All leading here. You think yourself so clever, mister, better'n all us townsfolk, with your fancy ways an' all. And now you've come to make sport of us. Them fires.'

'And that horse's head,' added Mrs. Longbottom. 'He's a sly one, all right.'

Several children started to whinny as she said this, but their voices were drowned in the exclamations about the fires and the lost haystacks and kegs of beer.

Wickham's habitual swagger faltered slightly, but he held his own.

'And what, pray, would be my motive for such ridiculous actions?'

'Ridiculous, are they?' responded Winterbottom. 'Ridiculous to you, with your money and your fine ways, I dare say, but folks like us have a living to make. It's not nothing, to lose all my kegs of beer.'

'Then perhaps, my dear sir, you should have licensed them and not produced them illegally,' said Wickham. 'You can have no recourse to the law when your own actions are outside of it.'

At this, the crowd was incensed, and Wickham, perhaps to divert their attention, rephrased his question.

'That's as may be, my good fellow, but why should I wish to burn your haystacks and your barns?'

The Bottoms fell silent and looked shiftily in my direction.

I stared back, not knowing what to say, as I am not quick on such occasions, and I was amazed to see Georgiana step to the front of the crowd.

'You may speak if you wish,' she said. 'It is not in my brother's nature to bear a grudge.'

There was silence for a moment. No one was accustomed to Georgiana putting herself forward in this way. Indeed, she looked quite shocked at her own temerity, and would have retreated behind Elizabeth, but my wife held her hand and patted her gently on the arm, and my sister stood her ground.

'Well, miss,' began Sally Shufflebottom, ' 'appen you won't know, but when your brother were a lad, Mr. Wickham 'ere made us all burn your brother's little boats. He said if we didn't, he'd tell your pa we'd been eating apples in the orchard at Pemberley. And we burned the boats, though we felt right bad about it, and ever since, we thought we should tell you, sir, and when Mr. Wickham come here a few months back, we told him it were time to come clean. All water under the bridge, an' all. We're all growed now, and we don't want no trouble. And then the fires started.'

'And we reckon,' continued Frederick Shufflebottom, 'as 'ow Mr. Wickham here is trying to warn us off speaking to you. We reckon he knows he won't get no more money from you once you know the truth.'

Wickham looked desperate, as well he might, but he realised he was outnumbered. The townsfolk were advancing on him, and he knew as well as any of us the penalty for arson.

I stepped forward.

'Thank you for your honesty,' I told the Bottoms. 'Yes, I do remember the boats, and the episode has haunted me these many years. I became a solitary child, fearful of other boys, and found it difficult to mix with others. It gave me a reputation for haughtiness, which, though partially deserved, was but a small part of my character. I am glad to know we can now put this incident behind us and live together in harmony.' I turned to Wickham. 'A harmony which you, sir, will not disrupt. If I ever hear of your presence in this vicinity again, know that we have enough evidence for you to be dealt with most severely by the law. Now take your horse and go!'

The Bottoms cheered, the other townsfolk jeered, and Wickham jumped on his horse and disappeared. He would not trouble us again.

As we rode home, I smiled approvingly at Georgiana.

'I must congratulate you, sister, on speaking up in this way. Especially after all you have suffered at the hands of that scoundrel Wickham.'

Her cheeks were a little pinker than usual as she looked up at me on Phoenix and replied, 'I said you would not bear a grudge, and I know you no longer hold their childish misdemeanours against the Bottoms. But in truth, you are not the only one in the family, my dear brother, whose good opinion cannot be regained, once it is lost. I have plenty more punishments in store for Mr. Wickham, if ever he shews his face here again. And I will protect my dearest Lizzy, if she should set ever so many fires against my dear brother's tormentors.'

⌒

That night, I spoke about this to Lizzy as we were preparing for bed.

'Does Georgiana suppose you lit the fires?' I asked.

'She implied as much,' replied my dear wife. 'But for a long time I supposed she set the fires herself. She has often confided in me a desire to take revenge on injustice, and when little William's hobby-horse was broken she was very sad and plotted all manner of schemes. Several times I have seen her quit the house at night and come back hours later when she thought she was unobserved.'

'And yet you were there to witness her return?' I asked.

'It is possible,' she replied. 'But tell me, is this mask I found in your closet in any way connected to the masked avenger?'

'It is possible,' I conceded.

'And the cloak and hat?'

'Again, it is possible,' I said.

'And if I were to tell you a family called Roebottom has recently returned to the town? Mrs. Reynolds tells me the man is around your age. Would his haystack be in danger?'

I thought carefully. The wrongs of the past had been righted, and I had no wish to arouse suspicion now Wickham was gone.

'I think,' I said, 'that his haystack would be safe.'

'That is a pity,' said Elizabeth. 'I had a great desire to see you once more in the mask and cape.'

'That can be arranged,' I said, starting to remove my waistcoat and jacket.

'But not the short drawers outside the breeches,' she warned me. 'That style will never be even tolerably acceptable, even among avengers of justice. It is perfectly ridiculous.'

'And the wet shirt?' I asked, gently stroking her bare shoulders. 'It was more than tolerably acceptable last time you saw it.'

'The wet shirt may stay,' she said. 'Only imagine, Mr. Darcy. Future generations may come to regard you as the instigator of a new fashion in casual attire.'

I did not believe her. Personally, I thought the wearing of short drawers outside the breeches had much to be said for it as a look suggestive of superior powers, while the wet shirt would have no attractions to any one. But my wife is often proved to be right.

CHAPTER 6

ANNE DE BOURGH – A WOMAN OF MEANS

I was initially discomfited by my cousin Fitzwilliam's marriage, but, on further reflection, I was not a little relieved. I had no desire to remove to the wilds of Derbyshire, far from the trappings of civilisation to which I was accustomed.

My mother, Lady Catherine, is of the firm opinion I am of a sickly disposition, and I do not wish to disillusion her. It is true my constitution is not as strong as that of some other young ladies, but I have benefited from the mask of sickness to shelter from my mother's overriding opinions. It is this mask that has furnished me with the excuse of abandoning any musical duties, with my continual protest that I am too ill to practise. Likewise, I have been able to elude the nauseating rides and hunts which my mother finds so stimulating, and was able to avoid being presented at court, with all the humiliations an overbearing mother could furnish on such an occasion.

My life, in truth, has been comfortable in material posses-
sions, but my mind has been greatly burdened by my mother's
interference, and I have not formerly dared to oppose her.
You may imagine my mingled shock and admiration when
I witnessed Elizabeth Bennet's boldness. How I longed to
join her procession in support of women's education. I often
wished I had such a strong character, but I feared that if I
disobeyed or displeased my mother, she would remove my
name from her will and I would be left without an inheritance.
I had seen how obdurate my mother was when she took
against a person, as she did with Elizabeth Bennet, and it
occurred to me that, should I cross my mother in any way,
she might just as well leave her estate to the horses in her
stables as to me, her ungrateful daughter. My only solace
was to spend time with my kindly companion, Miss Bishop.

Miss Bishop entered my mother's employ after Mrs.
Jenkinson departed. Mrs. Jenkinson was exceedingly fussy
and dull. Before her, my governess was Mrs. Younge, whom
I liked even less. I was very pleased when she was dismissed.
I will admit, a little subterfuge and exaggeration on my part
influenced that outcome. Nevertheless, it was Mrs. Younge
who taught me the skills that maintained my interest and
gave me a purpose long after her departure—she taught me
to play at cards.

When Miss Bishop arrived, she was ignorant of the
delights of the card-table, having never played any thing
more stimulating than lottery, a most unsatisfactory game of
pure chance. Over time, however, I taught her many different
games, including macao, commerce and unlimited loo. We
played every day, and when I was required to join in my

mother's pools of quadrille, I observed how it was possible to profit from a knowledge of gaming techniques. I have an excellent memory and am able to recall without difficulty which cards have been played. And despite my fragile appearance, I am not averse to taking risks. I therefore anticipated with pleasure our trips to Bath and the opportunities these afforded me to join the greater variety of gaming-tables there.

Our visit to Bath after my cousin Fitzwilliam's wedding was perhaps a little more subdued than in previous years. I say this on my mother's account. I was perfectly content, but she would have it that I was sorely disappointed that her wishes for my marriage had been flouted. She discoursed unceasingly on the unhappiness of Fitzwilliam's match, and obliged me to wear the most ridiculous head-dress of ostrich feathers, to shew I was undaunted by his marriage and was myself still marriageable. I could not care two figs about being marriageable, since I had not met any one I should wish to marry, but my mother wasted no time in introducing me to the most disagreeable men, all of whom she deemed suitable owing to the size of their estates. I had lately been introduced by Miss Bishop to a volume detailing the memoirs of a woman of pleasure named Fanny Hill, and so it was no longer the size of the men's estates that interested me, but it was hard to escape my mother's company. The only time I was not under her watchful eye was when she was engaged in a pool of quadrille and I was permitted to sit apart from her.

My first exploits at the gaming-table were very circumspect. I took no risks and was careful not to win too frequently. I profited from my mother's short-sightedness to sit at the far end of the room, away from her eagle observation, and played most days with the same little group of ladies and gentlemen. There were two couples, comprising Mr. and Mrs. Hurst, and Jane and Charles Bingley. There was Jane's sister Catherine, whom they called Kitty, and a soldier friend of hers called Mr. Denny. And there was a dashing young clergyman named Henry. The Bingleys played a gentle and rather insipid game, apologising frequently, as though they were afraid to win. Indeed, Jane would not stake any thing at all, and under her watchful eye Mr. Bingley would risk no more than a few shillings. Mr. Hurst was more alert than I had supposed from the other occasions on which I had met him, but he would keep falling asleep when we played after lunch, and his wife was more interested in playing on the pianoforte than in playing at cards, and had to be reminded frequently when it was her turn. Kitty giggled and chattered constantly with Denny, and the two of them seldom won a round. Henry was my keenest competitor. Losing to him was not difficult, the more so because I was distracted by his handsome dark eyes and tall well-made figure. His only distraction was to look sharply around the room every few minutes, as though anxious to avoid some one. When his attention was on the cards, however, he displayed an unfailing memory and was quick to spot any wrongful behaviour in others. I realised I would have to be very careful and try very hard if I were to win a game in his presence.

After our first week in Bath, I called Miss Bishop aside and spoke to her about Henry.

'What do you notice about him?' I asked. 'Is he a good player? Is he concealing any thing?'

'I think,' said she, 'that he is concealing much. I observed that often when he seems only to have three cards in his hand, he has another card hid beneath them. And on more than one occasion, I have spotted a card hid in his sleeve.'

'There,' I exclaimed. 'I thought he was not playing openly. But I know how we can remedy this and take back his winnings. And punish him handsomely into the bargain.'

My mother also questioned me about my afternoon distractions.

'With whom do you play?' she asked.

I opened my mouth to reply, but she continued, 'With the Bingleys and the Hursts, of course. I suppose they are all very well. Are there any other players?'

'There is Jane's sister Kitty, a young soldier, and a young clergyman.'

She sniffed. 'They are beneath your status. I hope you do not pay them much attention. I may have need of you at quadrille. I will call you at once if one of my party is absent. And pray take care of your ostrich feather bandeau. It is worth a considerable amount of money.'

⁓

The next day, I waited outside the room until my mother had commenced her game, anxious lest she summon me to make up the number of players. Then I joined my table and sat opposite to Henry. Miss Bishop sat a little behind him.

'You are very merry today, Miss de Bourgh,' said Henry, adjusting his clergyman's cravat and smiling his broad smile.

'Indeed I am, sir,' I said. 'For it is a pleasure to play at cards with such a distinguished group.'

The Bingleys were cooing to each other, the Hursts were loudly disparaging last night's dinner, and Kitty and Denny were giggling at some joke.

Henry smiled again. 'Indeed. They are very distinguished. But I think that *you* are a more interesting player, Miss de Bourgh. Shall we raise the stakes for our game today? What say you?'

'I say that is an excellent idea,' I countered.

We gained the attention of the others, and our play commenced. The Bingleys were quickly forced to quit the game, which they did with great good nature, leaving a large pile of gaming-chips on the table. Kitty was next to finish, and did so with less good grace, staying only because she wanted to observe Denny's progress. Mrs. Hurst left next, and then Denny had to throw down his hand. Now there were only myself and Henry and Mr. Hurst. A glance at Miss Bishop was sufficient to shew me that not only Henry, but Mr. Hurst, had hidden cards in their hands. I kept my counsel. I knew which cards had been played and which were necessary for me to win. I smiled at Miss Bishop, and she scratched her left cheek with two fingers. So Henry had the knave of hearts. Then she rubbed her right cheek with her thumb. Mr. Hurst had the queen of clubs. I raised my left eyebrow to indicate the game was ours. In this manner, I was able to win the following three games. Then it was time to stop for the afternoon.

Mr. Hurst was in a very ill humour, but Henry regarded me closely as we parted.

'I must congratulate you on a most hard-fought game, Miss de Bourgh,' he said, his eyes twinkling. 'I look forward to playing again tomorrow.'

His gaze wandered across the room to the table where my mother was playing quadrille, and I thought he blanched a little, but he took his leave of me cordially enough.

I gathered my winnings and concealed them in Miss Bishop's reticule. Next time we would need a larger receptacle.

On the morrow, I spent the morning parading the streets of Bath with my mother. She belittled each person we encountered, and though I longed to examine the fashions in one of the little shops on Milsom-street that Kitty had recommended, my mother would not allow it, saying only that she would have a new dress made for me by her dress-maker when we returned home, and she would choose the muslin herself, as I would not know which colour was the most suitable for my pale complexion. I remained silent, as I had always found remonstrance was useless, but I eagerly anticipated the afternoon's card game.

Later, my group was again united around the table. The weather was warm, and this inclined the ladies to use their fans, which furnished an additional weapon in the secret exchanges between Miss Bishop and myself. If she drew her fan across her forehead, it meant we were being watched. If she tapped the fan to her right cheek, it meant I was likely to lose. I played unremarkably to start with, losing a few tricks and a little money. Then the stakes were raised and I started to win again. At one point, Henry whirled around in his seat to look at Miss Bishop, but she was studiously fanning herself and murmuring about the great heat in the room, a complaint that found echo in the voices of the other ladies at our table. The amount of money bet upon the game rose and rose. Kitty and the Bingleys retired. Denny and Mrs. Hurst played a little longer, until they lost handsomely. Now there were thousands of guineas at stake, and it was all I could do to contain my excitement. There remained only myself, Mr. Hurst and Henry. I debated whether I should allow Henry to win the game and thereby divert suspicion, but I did not think he would be able to prove any thing against me so far, and, after a coded signal from Miss Bishop, I raised my left eyebrow and allowed myself the joy of victory. Mr. Hurst looked very sour, and Henry was less congratulatory than previously. He again glanced at my mother and then opened his mouth to speak, but closed it, took up his hat and left.

Miss Bishop and I discussed the game in my room before dinner that evening.

'I think Henry has noticed our little signals,' I said. 'Perhaps the use of the fan is too obvious.'

She shook her head. 'I am sure he was not quick enough to see me. But I think he suspects all is not as it seems. It might be better if you do not win tomorrow.'

I was unwilling to lose, but I conceded the wisdom of her advice. That evening at dinner, my mother and I sat with the Bingleys and the Hursts. My mother was loath to let Kitty join us, but Jane Bingley would not hear of her sitting elsewhere, and so I sat opposite to Kitty. She is delicate in constitution, like myself, but rather empty-headed, always casting her eyes around her for men in uniform. And yet, she was friendly, and as my mother had evidently taken against her, purely due to her own prejudices, I was more kindly disposed towards her.

'Do you not think,' she whispered to me, 'that Henry is very handsome?'

'I suppose he is,' I replied.

'I think he is not such a good sport as Denny, but his looks are very striking, even though he is a clergyman. I like a man with dark hair. He has something of Mr. Darcy about him. Oh. I am sorry. I did not mean . . .'

'Pray, do not concern yourself,' I said. 'It is true I might once have looked favourably on Mr. Darcy, but now I am quite content for him to have married your sister Elizabeth. I would not want to live in Derbyshire!'

'I agree entirely,' said Kitty. 'Then you must marry Henry. Only, leave the ostrich feathers behind you. They are quite alarming.'

My mother's attention was elsewhere, so I turned to Kitty and permitted myself to giggle quietly with her. I had always thought being an only child was a lonely thing, and had wished for sisters. Now I had the delight of exchanging girlish thoughts with Miss Bishop and with Kitty. My life's horizons were broadening daily. I looked over at Henry. He was seated far from us and seemed to be avoiding looking in our direction. I supposed he had other people to occupy him. The woman next to him was very pretty and fashionably dressed. And he was only a clergyman; my mother would never approve such a match. She might even disinherit me, were I to marry some one she had not chosen herself. But thanks to my card playing, I was becoming a young lady of some means, and in the future, who knew what match I might care to make of my own accord?

The next day I played poorly, though not so badly as to arouse suspicion. Henry won the first game, and Miss Bishop told me later he had cheated several times. I did not like that turn of events, and so I permitted myself to win on the next two occasions. At the end of the day, Henry touched my elbow and led me aside.

'A word in your ear, if you will,' he said, smiling roguishly, his dark eyes flashing in his handsome face.

I left my ostrich feather bandeau behind, praying that some one would take it, and followed him to an empty table, hopeful of a more intimate dialogue away from the crowd. Once on our own, however, he dropped his smile and was most direct.

'I know that you and Miss Bishop are cheating,' he said. 'If you do not desist, I will make your conduct known to the others on our table and to the room at large. I hardly think Lady Catherine de Bourgh's daughter will want to be known as a deceiver. What would your mother say?'

He looked in her direction, but turned away again hastily when she raised her head.

I had never been in a situation such as this before. I was not greatly bothered about my behaviour being exposed on our table, the others being too indolent to pay much attention, but I was frightened at the thought of my mother's reaction. And I was angry that my initial assessment of his character had proved too hasty. He was no longer in the slightest bit attractive to me.

'And you, sir,' I said. 'You yourself are cheating. You have cards hid up your sleeve, and you obscure other cards in your hand to your own advantage.'

I held his gaze.

'The d*** I do,' he said. 'You minx.'

We regarded each other for fully two minutes, until his gaze dropped.

'I can see we are evenly matched,' he said. 'What say you we work together and divide the winnings?'

It was a tempting possibility, and I could not see an immediate alternative, so I acquiesced. Alas, my ostrich feathers were still on our card-table, and I was obliged to take the bandeau back with me to my room.

For the rest of the season, Henry and I conspired to win nearly every match, and to share the proceeds. We played against people on different tables and were careful to lose occasionally to allay suspicions. To start with, we divided the money evenly, but then Henry began to take more than his fair portion. When I raised the matter with him, he threatened to expose my own behaviour. This was not to be borne.

Miss Bishop and I discussed the situation, and she made known to me a fact of which I was hitherto unaware. Henry was familiar to my mother. This must be the reason why he looked frequently in her direction. She, however, being short-sighted, did not notice him. I asked Miss Bishop how she knew of Henry and my mother's acquaintance, but she would say only that he had once been to Rosings, but had left precipitately, and would have no desire to meet my mother again. At last we thought I might manage a way out of the situation.

The next day we sat down to play. It was the final afternoon of the season, and we would all be leaving the following morning. The stakes were higher than ever, and I stood to win thousands of guineas, if only I received my fair share. I sat opposite to Henry; Miss Bishop stood behind him. My mother had made sure I was wearing my hated bandeau with the ridiculous ostrich plumes. Henry arranged his clergyman's cloak on the back of his seat and we commenced play.

This time I did not look at Henry. I allowed myself to win solely through my own skills, with a little help from Miss Bishop and her fan. Henry glared at me, and when we paused for refreshment, he spoke to me openly.

'If you continue in this way, Miss de Bourgh, I shall be forced to denounce your conduct to the assembly.'

'You may denounce me all you wish, sir,' I said. 'I have no fear of you, for I have done nothing wrong.'

I spoke thus, with a firm voice, but I confess my heart was a-tremble. I laid aside my winnings, and we exchanged seats and commenced a new game. This time I played without artifice, and without the benefit of Miss Bishop, who had quitted the room. I allowed Henry to win until we had nearly finished the game, and then I played a card which put me in a good way to win the whole set and become mistress of the ten thousand pounds he had staked. At this, he stood up, looked majestically around him and opened his mouth to make a pronouncement.

But he was interrupted by the arrival of Miss Bishop and a constable.

'There!' she exclaimed. 'That is the man. He has been cheating at cards. And if you look, you will find he has a card even now concealed in his sleeve.'

Henry's face was all astonishment and anger.

'No, sir,' he said. 'This is unjust. It is that woman who is to be arrested.'

And he pointed at my side of the table, where, but a moment before, I had been sitting with a hand of cards. But alas for him, the seat was empty, the ostrich feather bandeau drooped on my chair, and I was nowhere to be seen. Only, if he had looked more carefully, he would have spotted a small, slim figure, in a clerical cloak and hat, making their way to the exit.

The constable laid a firm hand on Henry's shoulder.

'Come with me now, sir, or it will be the worse for you.'

Henry's voice rose. 'No, no,' he shouted. 'Do not touch me!'

The hall fell silent, and my mother, seated at the other end, turned to look at him. As I peeped round the door, I swear her face lit up and his face fell even further, when she cried, 'Mr. Stephens. How happy I am to see you again!'

The room was in an uproar. Henry was protesting his innocence, my mother was advancing on him with arms outstretched and a firmness of step that shewed an even greater firmness of purpose, and Kitty and Denny were in a flutter of mirth and excitement. Eventually my mother persuaded the constable that no untoward conduct had taken place, and Henry was released into her care. His steps dragged as he left the room with her, but he could not deny she had saved him.

I returned Henry's cloak to his chair and he collected it later after some private intercourse with my mother. The clerical hat I kept as a trophy, and, happily for me, the ostrich feather bandeau had disappeared in the general disturbance.

I do not know which caused Henry the most discomfit—the legal accusation or my mother's conduct—but we were not troubled by him again. Miss Bishop enlightened me as to the situation that led him to quit Rosings so suddenly, and I heard much later that he was gone to take up a living in Aberdeen and never again ventured south of Edinburgh.

My mother was in a heightened state when we left for home the next day, and once our journey had started, she accosted me in the carriage.

'I hope, Anne, you have not made a fool of yourself in Bath.'

I thought back to my time there. I had proved a skill that gave me both pleasure and a means of providing a living. I had made a friend in Kitty. I had, which was new for me, gained self-respect. Where once I was cowed, now I had confidence. Where once I feared a lack of wealth, now I had a fund of guineas that was but the start of a new future.

My mother continued in her imperious way. 'Mr. Stephens is a pleasant enough man, but he is well below your station. You must take more care with whom you socialise.'

My eyes no longer downcast, I looked my mother full in the face. 'I might say the same to you, madam. Do not think I am unaware of your relations with Mr. Stephens, and of the manner in which he quit Rosings.'

'Impudence,' she replied. 'You will speak to me with respect, Anne, or I will disown you.'

'You may disown me as you will,' I said. 'I have the means to support myself now, and I will not be dictated to, by you or any one else. Not now, not ever.'

My mother opened her mouth in shock. I raised my left eyebrow. Miss Bishop smiled behind her fan. And for the first time in my life, my mother was silent.

Chapter 7

Jane Bingley – A Den of Iniquity

The baby fox regarded us piteously. Its right hind paw was enclosed in the trap and it was unable to move. In the distance, we heard the baying of hounds and the sound of the huntsmen's horns. I stroked the little animal gently and attempted to prise apart the metal springs that held it fast, but I could not do it. The fox-cub was gasping, trying to draw breath.

'Mamma, what can we do?' asked Eliza, my eldest, named for my sister Lizzy. Her face was anxious as she cradled the little fox in her lap, heedless of the blood soaking into her dress. She is six years old, and like her aunt, she has an independent spirit.

I wished Lizzy were with us. She is so brave and resourceful, and I feel that I move a little in her shadow. But Lizzy was not there, so I must shift for myself, and I had Eliza to consider too. I knew she wanted to help me, so I pushed down on one side of the trap.

'Hold this down, Eliza,' I said. 'I will open the other side.' She tugged at the metal, but her fingers were not strong enough to hold it.

I looked around me and found a stout stick with which I kept one part of the trap open while I pulled on the other. The iron jaws parted and the fox-cub was free, but it could not run away. It lay in Eliza's lap, panting. There was a great deal of blood on her dress now, and I knew we had to get away before the hunt reached us.

In the distance, I heard Lady Catherine's fox-hounds baying and the huntsmen shouting, their horses' hooves thudding across the fields. I was thankful my dear Charles did not indulge in this blood-thirsty sport. I wrapped the fox-cub in my kerchief and took Eliza's hand. We hastened away from the hunt, crossing field after field until we found ourselves in Lady Catherine's stables at Rosings, our faces glowing with the warmth of exercise.

The stable-boy, when I ran him to earth, was unbelieving. 'They's bad, they is, ma'am,' he said. 'It's a littl'un now, but you wait. You don't want to see what he'll do to your chickens.'

I knew he was right—an adult fox can destroy a chicken coop in minutes—but this was a baby, and I had to help him. The stable-boy brought us a bucket of warm water, and I shewed Eliza how to wash the little fox's leg and bind it with some fresh cloths. It was a very small animal, and when I set it on the floor it did not run away, only snuggled against our legs and looked up at us beseechingly. I prayed Lady Catherine would not find him.

After Lizzy and Fitzwilliam's marriage, Lady Catherine did not want any of us to visit, and we did not want to visit her.

What she termed her frankness and we termed her rudeness were such that I thought we would never see her again, but by degrees, and to satisfy her curiosity about Lizzy's fitness as a wife, she condescended to wait on the party at Pemberley, and they in turn began to visit her at Rosings. Charles and I would sometimes accompany them, as it made a change for our children, and they loved to visit their Gardiner relatives in London on the way.

We have four living children, and I hope we shall have many more. Eliza is the eldest. She is bright and merry like her Aunt Lizzy, and always running into mischief. Little Charles is like his Grandfather Bennet, with a dry sense of humour unusual in a four-year-old. Cassie is two years old and sings like an angel. Baby Walter was still-born, and I nearly died giving birth to him. How hard it is to be a mother at such times. Baby Maria is all smiles and dimples in the daytime and a waking terror at night, but I am happy every time I hear her voice, and Miss Jones, our nursery-maid, is a great comfort and help to me.

This time, we had arrived a few days before Lizzy and Fitzwilliam, who were making a visit to Cambridge, and we had the dubious pleasure of Lady Catherine's unadulterated attention. It was on this occasion I learned about Lady Catherine's hatred of foxes.

'I cannot even bear to see one,' she told us at dinner that evening. 'I am sure I do not understand why any one would want to keep the brush at the end of a hunt. Disgusting creatures. Vermin! I would not care if every fox in England were hunted down.'

'You are concerned for the livestock they kill, Lady Catherine?' enquired Charles.

'Indeed, I care nothing about the livestock. The villagers might have plenty of chickens, if they would listen to my schemes for improving their animal husbandry. They have only to build better fences around their poultry yards.'

'I have heard, ma'am, that foxes will often dig a long way under a fence to steal the ducks within,' said Charles.

'You have heard?' She glared at him. 'Pray, since when did hearing prove any thing? Where are the sworn facts? If a farmer is too lazy to protect his herds and his poultry, he has only himself to blame.'

I thought that if a landowner were too lazy to protect their farmers, they might blame only themselves when there were no chickens left to produce eggs for supper, but unlike Lizzy, I was too timid to voice my thoughts. Instead, I rose to take my leave.

'Good night, Lady Catherine,' I said. 'Charles, pray do not hurry. I know you enjoy your game of whist.'

'I wish you would join us, Jane,' said Charles.

'My dear, I will join you another night. I am still tired from Maria's waking.'

'We are all tired from Maria's waking,' said Lady Catherine. 'Jane, you look quite fagged. And you have not washed your hands properly. Is that blood on your finger? I will have my maid help you. What is that in your reticule? Have you brought your child's doll to the table?'

'No, Lady Catherine,' I said. 'Only, the nights are cold, and I have brought my fur muff in case my fingers become chilled. But I will retire now.'

I went to the nursery, where I placed my bag on the table and opened it with care. Eliza was still awake and she raced to join me.

'How is our little patient, mamma?' she asked.

Little Reynard peered up at us from my reticule. He had been asleep, but now he drank thirstily from a cup of milk I had obtained for Eliza. Then he crawled to the edge of the table and put out a paw, as though to leap to the floor, but he drew back. Evidently he was still not strong enough.

'I know,' said Eliza. 'I have the very thing.'

She scurried into the nursery and fetched a little doll's bed. The fox-cub looked snug amid the cushions and blankets. Our nursery-maid, Miss Jones, was enraptured.

'He is like a little puppy,' she said. 'I will keep him with me tonight if you like, and Eliza shall help me feed him tomorrow.'

~

The next morning, we took Reynard for a walk. Miss Jones said he had awakened in the night, and she had played games with him like a puppy, rolling a little ball and petting his back, but now he wanted to sleep. I bade Miss Jones get some rest while the children and I walked in the woods. I carried baby Maria and Eliza took Reynard in a scarf tied to her body, while Charlie and Cassie ran and hid among the trees. I did not want them to know about Reynard, lest they announce his presence to Lady Catherine, but it was hard work to distract them.

'Shall we not tell papa and the others about our fox?' asked Eliza.

'By and bye,' I said.

'I hope we can rescue many baby foxes,' said Eliza. 'Reynard shall be our first, and when we go home we shall look for others.'

We stayed away from the house, but on our return we were met near the shrubbery by Lady Catherine. She was talking to Mr. Mellors, the gamekeeper, but she interrupted her conversation to inspect us.

'I am surprised, Eliza,' she said, looking at the scarf with the little body hidden inside it, tightly wrapped to Eliza's body. 'You are six years old. Do you still take an interest in dolls?'

'She does indeed, Lady Catherine,' I said. 'It is usual for a little girl to like her dolls.'

Lady Catherine sniffed. 'I let my daughter Anne have a doll, but only while she was too young to ride a horse. A child should not be indulged.'

'In any case, it is not a doll,' said Eliza. Like her Aunt Lizzy, she is not easily intimidated.

'Then what is it you have there?' asked Lady Catherine. 'I demand to know.'

A small red and white snout protruded a little from the green scarf. Charlie and Cassie exclaimed in wonder.

'A puppy, a puppy!' they shouted.

'It is a puppy,' I said to Lady Catherine. 'A fox-hound. It was lame, and we are caring for it.'

My statement was correct in almost all its particulars. I was all concern that Mellors would betray us, but he only winked at me. I think Lady Catherine was not his favourite employer.

Lady Catherine sniffed once more. 'I suppose that is a good enough sentiment. It will earn its keep by and bye when it joins the hunt. Do not bring it indoors. And you may like to know, Mrs. Bingley, that Cook tells me the hens are laying very well just now, and we shall have cake for tea. You see, your husband's assertions are not at all correct.'

After looking meaningfully at me, she walked back to the house.

'I hope 'ee know what 'ee's about,' said Mellors. 'Remember, her ladyship don't like foxes. 'Twould be a pity if one got into the house now, wouldn't it, after her being so rude to you, an' all?'

And he went on his way, chuckling.

That evening, the household was awakened by screams from Lady Catherine's apartments. We hastened to the scene and found her ladyship in her night-dress, her hair in a state of wild disarray.

'There!' she exclaimed. 'There was a fox, just there! A small one. It is under the bed. You must remove it at once.'

Charles and I searched for half an hour, but I knew there was no fox to be found. I had made sure he was safely back in the nursery after his little excursion. In the end, Lady Catherine repaired to another chamber, and we all fell asleep.

'What do you suppose happened?' Charles asked me in the morning. 'I am certain it was her imagination. There is no fox in the house.'

'I am sure you are right, my dear,' I said.

And he was correct. There was no fox in the house now. Early that morning, Eliza and I had driven with Reynard in the phaeton to a culvert some distance away and released him. After retiring a safe distance and waiting in the cold for what seemed like hours, we saw a vixen approach and take Reynard into a patch of gorse. Three other little fox-cubs were gambolling around them. Evidently, that was where they had their den.

Lady Catherine was in deep dudgeon about the fox in her chamber, although we all assured her the creature existed only in her fancy. At dinner that night, she announced there would be another hunt meeting in two days' time.

I took my courage in both hands. 'You do not need a hunt, Lady Catherine,' I said. 'There cannot be more foxes here. And you said yourself, the hens are safe. They have laid a great many eggs.'

Lady Catherine looked at me in surprise. She had not been used to have any one disagree with her. 'The hens are safe because we hunt the foxes. You must know that. The hunt will proceed.'

⁓

Charles disliked hunting as much as I. He had seen men and horses die when jumping over ditches and walls, and although he did not like foxes, he did not regard chasing them as sport. Consequently, he did not take part in the hunt. Instead, we planned a day with the children, far from the bustle and noise. However, little Charlie wanted to see the grand hunt uniforms and the horses, so we took the children to see them before they set off. Many riders seemed to have gathered merely to display their skill, and some of the farmers and other country-dwellers looked on surlily, anxious about the damage to their fields.

'I would not want to go with them, mamma,' said Eliza. 'I like the dogs, but I want our little Reynard to be well. He will escape, won't he?'

Charles took her hand. 'Why do you call the fox your little Reynard, Eliza? Is he your pet? Ho ho. But do not worry. I am sure he will outwit these addlepated hunters. Come. Let us go for a ride.'

It was only at the very last moment that I was prevented from joining my dear family. Lady Catherine had departed with her huntsmen and hounds, and Charles and the children were assembled in front of the house, ready to mount the open carriage. At that moment, I put a hand to my forehead.

'My dear, are you quite well?' asked Charles.

'It is nothing,' I said. 'Only, I think perhaps it would be better if I stayed at home. I do not feel equal to the outing today.'

'Mamma, you must join us,' was on the lips of all my children, while baby Maria closed her eyes and slept soundly in Miss Jones's arms.

'I am sorry, my dears,' I said. 'Papa will look after you.'

'Indeed I will,' said Charles. 'We shall look for horse chestnuts and we shall have a game of conkers when we return.'

'Horse chestnuts?' I said. 'That is new. I had thought you would need snail shells for that game.'

'That is true,' said Charles. 'But I will invent a new game with horse chestnuts. It is the season, and they will make much prettier conkers.'

'Conkers. Hurray!' cried Eliza and Charlie, and Cassie

sang, 'Conkies, conkies.' It did not take much to distract them, and their father was as excited as they to be driving out on this fine day.

Miss Jones returned to the house with Maria. I waved the carriage off, and when it was quite out of sight I went to the stables, where Lady Catherine's daughter Anne kept her phaeton and ponies. It did not take long for the stable-boy to harness them for me. When he was gone, I dropped a sack and a piece of string onto the seat of the phaeton, then I followed the direction the hunt had taken. I did not quite know what I should do, but I could not remain inactive.

As I followed the imprint of hooves in a muddy field, I heard the tally-ho and bugle calls of the riders and the barking of the fox-hounds. They were approaching the culvert where I had released the baby fox. I did not expect to find it waiting for me outside its den, but an idea came to me. I stood near the patch of gorse and held the sack open, then I called gently, 'Reynard.' There was a shuffling noise and a crackling of sticks. Then, very cautiously, a long, pointed nose poked its way out into the open. I swear it was Reynard's mother. I stood very still, with the sack open, while the two ponies snorted and shuffled in dismay. The vixen approached warily, as though appraising me, but as the noise of the hunt drew nearer, it seemed to prompt her to action. She disappeared into the hole, then reappeared carrying a fox-cub by the scruff of its neck. She looked at me again and dropped the cub carefully into the sack. Then she disappeared, and I was about to leave when she came back with another cub. She did this four times; then she gave me a last, haunted look and turned and fled, through the gorse patch and over the stream.

My ponies were trembling now at the sound of the bugles and the dogs, only a few fields away. I fastened the string roughly around the opening of the sack, dropped the whole onto the seat of the phaeton, and returned to Rosings as fast as I could, crossing several brooks on the way so the dogs would lose our scent. The phaeton was too light for such treatment, and it was all I could do to keep my seat and maintain my hold on the reins and the sack with the wriggling fox-cubs. I was soon covered in dust, and we slowed our pace considerably as we progressed. I am sure Lizzy would have managed it better, but I hung on, and by and bye we reached Rosings Park.

Lady Catherine and her hunting party guests were still absent when I entered the grounds, and my own family was not yet returned. I was loath to leave the fox-cubs in the stables, lest Mellors or the stable-boy discover them, so I carried the sack up to the house. Four baby foxes were too many to hide in the nursery, but there were a number of empty guest apartments in a far wing of the house, and I made a little nest with blankets in one of them, beneath a bed. The fox-cubs were fast asleep. I obtained a chamber pot and filled it with water for the animals, then I quitted the room. My plan was to release the fox-cubs in the grounds of Rosings when the hunt guests were gone and the hounds were locked away for the night.

No sooner had I quitted the guest room than my family returned, the children capering with the joy of their expedition.

'Look, mamma,' said Eliza. 'We have found so many horse chestnuts. And mine are the biggest. See? Papa says he will make a hole in each one and thread it with a piece of string. Then we can play conkers.'

I smiled at her. 'Your papa has invented a new game.'

'Indeed I have,' said Charles. 'But are you quite well now, Jane? It was a pity you could not come. We had a capital time.' His eyes shone, and I think he enjoyed finding horse chestnuts quite as much as the children did.

'I am quite well now, my dear,' I said. And without a doubt, I felt very well indeed.

I was obliged to tell Miss Jones about the fox-cubs, as I needed some one to watch them when I was absent at dinner. I was thankful that foxes are nocturnal creatures and would not stir till the evening, and I planned to remove them as soon as I could.

The talk at the dinner table was all of the disappointment of the hunt.

'Not a single fox,' said Lady Catherine. 'They are very sly creatures. I know there are several on my land, and our dogs almost caught them. We followed the hounds for miles and were close to running the vermin to ground, but it appears some one interfered.'

'How do you know there was a disruption, your ladyship?' I asked.

'My master of fox-hounds saw a fox in the distance, but it ran through a stream and the hounds lost the scent.'

'Then it was well for the fox,' I replied. 'And the fact that it could run fast does not imply any interference in the hunt from an outsider.'

She looked at me disdainfully. 'You are becoming very sure of your opinions, Mrs. Bingley. My men examined the ground, and they found a den and traces of several foxes, as well as hoof-prints and the marks of coach wheels nearby. It appears some one was involved in the fox's escape. Disrupting a hunt is iniquitous. I will see to it the criminal is brought to justice.'

I retired early again that night, and this time Charles accompanied me.

'Miss Sly!' he said, kissing me on the nose. 'I am pleased your head no longer aches, but I wonder, if I examined the phaeton and the ponies in the stables, would I find traces of mud, or even traces of fox?'

'You might,' I admitted.

'Capital!' he exclaimed. 'And the fox the other night?'

'I think he is back now with his brothers and sisters.'

'Why did you not tell me before?'

'I am sorry, my love. I was unhappy when Lady Catherine affronted you, and I did not want her to suspect your involvement. And now she has insulted me and Eliza too. I will not stand by while she slaughters these little creatures for her sport. Killing foxes has become a pastime for the wealthy, not a necessity for farmers.'

'You are right,' said Charles. 'Where once our local farmers complained of foxes stealing their chickens, now they are as likely to protest against their fields being trampled by huntsmen, or their lambs being killed by the surfeit of foxes brought in to satisfy the whims of blood-thirsty landowners such as Lady Catherine.'

I kissed him, and we went together to the guest bedroom. The little foxes were starting to become restless, and we could not keep them in the house any longer.

'We should take the fox-cubs outside and release them,' I said.

It took me a long time to coax them into the sack, but at last we were ready. We had no more string, the children having used it all for their game of conkers, but we twisted the top of the bag to keep it closed.

'Pray, allow me,' said Charles. He swung the sack onto his shoulder and we set off down the stairs.

It was unfortunate the children had abandoned their conker game so near the drawing-room. We were walking quietly to avoid detection by the whist players and port drinkers, when Charles slipped on a pile of horse chestnuts. His feet went from under him, and he let go of the sack and reached for a large urn on a plinth to steady himself. The vase fell and smashed into a thousand pieces, and the terrified fox-cubs ran into the drawing-room.

All was confusion. Lady Catherine was standing on a chair, her skirts gathered around her ankles, shouting that this outrage must be stopped. The whist players were running for pokers and fire irons. The port drinkers were roused from their slumbers and were demanding to know what the d*** was happening.

I was very frightened for the fox-cubs, but I saw how the situation might be remedied. I held up the sack and approached the shadows beside the fireplace.

'Look there!' I exclaimed, pointing to the opposite corner of the room. Then I scooped four small logs into the sack while every one's attention was distracted. 'No, I was mistaken. See, they are in here.' And I held up the heavy sack and handed it to my husband. 'Charles,' I said, 'you must take these foxes away.'

'Destroy them!' said Lady Catherine. 'This is iniquitous. They must be killed this instant. Take them to the game-keeper's lodge. Mellors will dispose of them.'

Charles and I left the house and walked towards the game-keeper's cottage. Mellors answered the door in his breeches, his hair dishevelled. He looked annoyed at the disturbance.

'Wait there, Constance,' he shouted into the interior of his house. Then he came onto the step and closed the door behind him. 'Yes? What can I do for 'ee?'

'Lady Catherine sent you some wood,' I said, as Charles handed him the sack of logs, together with half a sovereign. 'I suppose you have not seen any foxes here?'

He winked at us. 'Only dead 'uns, ma'am. Ain't that right, sir?'

'Very right,' said Charles. 'I am sorry to have disturbed you.'

'No trouble, sir,' he said, going back into the cottage and closing the door.

Charles and I returned to the house. I thought I had seen the foxes run out of the drawing-room and down the steps to the lawn, but I could not be certain. Charles hastened to assure Lady Catherine the vermin were gone, and I went up to the children's rooms. Eliza rushed to greet me.

'Eliza. Are you still awake?' I stroked her tousled hair from her forehead.

'I heard a noise,' she said, 'and then I looked through the window. And mamma, I saw four baby foxes! Reynard brought his brothers and sisters to play. But they all ran away.' Her face fell.

'That is a very good thing, darling. It means the fox-cubs are safe.'

Her face brightened. I tucked her back into bed and went down stairs to join my husband.

'I have heard,' Lady Catherine was saying, 'that once a family of foxes enters a house, more foxes will follow.'

I took my courage in both hands. 'You have heard, Lady Catherine? Pray, since when did hearing prove any thing? Where are the sworn facts?'

She contemplated me for a moment. 'Mrs. Bingley, you are becoming as opinionated as your sister Elizabeth, and as silly as your mother. I am sorry to see it. Mr. Bingley, you must make sure your wife does not dominate you. I cannot abide an overbearing woman.'

Charles opened his mouth to reply, but I forestalled him.

'Lady Catherine,' I said, 'you have insulted me in every manner possible. I am proud to be known as having opinions. And when we return home, I shall continue to defend the rights of foxes against landowners like yourself.'

***

'My dear,' said Charles in bed that night, 'why do you ever doubt yourself?'

'I feel Lizzy is so much stronger than I,' I said. 'I often hold back my opinions. I am not as brave as Lizzy. I did not even go to her procession in Cambridge.'

'My darling, you were nearing the birth of our child. You could not go to her protest. But you are as brave as any one.'

'I am?' I asked.

He stroked my cheek. 'Are you really going to defend the rights of foxes?'

'Against landowners like Lady Catherine, yes.'

'I have heard,' said Charles, 'that once a resolve is taken, there is no turning back.'

'You have heard?' I murmured. 'Pray, since when did hearing prove any thing?'

'The proof is in the action,' he said. 'I am proud of you.'

'And Eliza,' I said. 'She was with me when we rescued little Reynard.'

'Then I am the happiest man in the world, and I will help my two little criminals with all my heart.'

'Are we criminals?' I asked.

'Not to me.'

'I think you are a little prejudiced,' I said. 'But I am glad you think I am as brave as Lizzy.'

'You are braver,' he said. 'She is not afraid to speak her mind, but you are afraid, and yet you still say and do what you know is right.'

He took me in his arms, and I put Lizzy's shadow firmly behind me and moved into the light of my own convictions.

Chapter 8

Catherine Bennet – A Dress Fit for a Queen

Our soldier friend Chamberlayne looked so pretty when my sister Lydia and I dressed him in my aunt's gown. Even his friends Denny and Wickham thought he was a girl and flirted with him shamelessly. And the strangest thing was, that even when Denny knew it was Chamberlayne, he still kept trifling with him. They called each other "queen" and said dressing up was a pleasant deed, and then they fell over themselves laughing.

But that was all before Lydia and Wickham were married. Now I do not see Lydia often, but I still went to Bath this season with my sister Jane and her husband Charles. Papa did not want me to go, but mamma persuaded him that Jane would look after me and there would not be any soldiers to flirt with. Only, they did not know Denny and Chamberlayne would be there.

The journey to Bath was very long. I read my beauty book, *The Mirror of the Graces*, and I asked that the window be kept open all the way, because I felt so sick in the carriage. But Jane and Charles were very kind and did not mind at all, and their children kept looking out of the window and exclaiming at every thing. They are nice children, but they are noisy. I will not have so many children. How do I know? I will tell you a secret.

When I was in Lydia's old bedroom, I found a book on her shelves about a lady who called herself a woman of pleasure. I was very surprised by the story, and I could not stop reading it. I cannot think why Lydia did not take it with her, but I suppose she left in a hurry when she eloped with Wickham. And so, this book taught me a lot of things about men and women, and now I know why papa is worried about soldiers. But he does not need to worry about Denny and Chamberlayne, for they would never take advantage of me.

Denny and I played at cards every day in Bath with Jane and Charles, and Charles's sister Mrs. Hurst and her husband, and Lady Catherine de Bourgh's daughter Anne, and a clergyman friend of hers, Mr. Stephens. I thought I should have died when I saw Lady Catherine, but she mostly ignored me, only she would keep suggesting remedies for my cough. I poured them into the flower-beds when she was not looking. I do not trust medications.

One day I went walking with Charles and Denny, and we passed an inn, and I heard Denny say to himself, 'That is a Molly House.' I asked Denny what he meant, but he would not tell me. I tried to see through the window, but the curtains were drawn. Then I saw two tall women go in, and Denny said, 'Nice stampers.' I looked where Denny was looking, and saw that the women had very big feet, and I thought that was what "stampers" meant, but he said he meant shoes, and it was true—they did have nice shoes.

I said to Denny, 'Why should we not dress you in woman's clothes and shew you to Anne de Bourgh and my sister Jane? It will be such sport. Do you not think so, Charles?'

'Capital fun,' said Charles. I knew he would like the idea. He is such an obliging fellow and he always loves a joke. 'But where shall we find a gown?' he asked. 'Denny is taller than you or Anne or Jane.'

'I will talk to Anne's companion, Miss Bishop,' I said. 'I am sure she will help us.'

~

That evening, when Lady Catherine was at the whist table instructing every one how to behave, Miss Bishop and Anne and Denny and I went into Lady Catherine's room and chose a gold evening dress with a silver pattern and white satin sleeves looped up with pearls. I would not wear it—it is so long it is not fashionable—but it was good for Denny, because Lady Catherine's shoes were all too small for him and the long dress would hide his feet. No one would see his stampers! We also borrowed a dark brown wig from Miss Bishop, with a bun at the back and curls around the face. It fitted Denny perfectly. And we borrowed some silk stockings and garters and a shawl and some long gloves that came up over the elbow, so the hair on his arms would not shew. Then we added some hoop ear rings and pearl necklaces. He looked so pretty, we could hardly wait to shew him to our friends, so we went at once to the Assembly Rooms and found Charles.

'Here is our new companion,' I said.

'Good Lord,' said Charles. 'I quite took you for a woman, Denny. Let us introduce you to Jane and the Hursts.'

So we went to their table, and no one recognised Denny. Such a joke! Then I could not keep from laughing, and Jane became suspicious, and in the end we told them all who Denny was. Jane was shocked at first, but then she laughed, and Mrs. Hurst looked like she did not know if she was eating a lemon or a strawberry, her expression changed back and forth so much. But Mr. Hurst looked very cross.

'D*** it, sir,' he said. 'It is a very bad thing to dress as a woman. You are a man, sir. This will not do. Are you not ashamed?'

But we all laughed and laughed.

⁓

The next day, Denny's friend Chamberlayne arrived, and we told him about our joke. We were at the Assembly Rooms and we pointed out Mr. Hurst, who was asleep in a chair.

'Upon my soul,' said Chamberlayne. 'The man is a hypocrite. I have seen him in London, strolling and caterwauling at the White Lion in Haymarket. It is very unfair of him to disrespect you, Denny.'

Well, I thought, if Mr. Hurst was caterwauling, that was a very loud thing to do. He must have been in liquor.

'And I saw him in the chapel,' said Chamberlayne.

I thought that was not too bad, though it was not as good as a church, but Chamberlayne said some one in the chapel should not criticise Denny, and I am sure he was right.

Denny and Chamberlayne said they would take revenge on Mr. Hurst for being so rude, so we plotted what to do, and Denny had a capital idea.

Two nights later, we borrowed some more clothes from Lady Catherine, and this time Chamberlayne put them on. He wore a ruby-coloured velvet robe, with velvet and white crêpe short sleeves, and a white crêpe dress underneath. The robe parted in the middle so you could see the dress. And we put a black wig on his head, with ribbons in the bun.

We searched *The Mirror of the Graces* for ideas for his face, and we set a nap on his cheek with a little bit of pomatum that had wax in it, and mixed it with carmine to make a perfect rouge. Now his cheeks were pink and we had not used any thing harmful. We were mindful of the Countess of Coventry, who died of wearing make-up full of lead. Then we drew a black line on the edges of his eyelids and put some Rigge's Liquid Bloom on his lips. It is made of Damask roses and it made his lips pink and shiny, so that I thought any one would want to kiss them, though I am sorry to say it has not happened to me yet when I wear it.

Chamberlayne looked at himself in the mirror and was very pleased. 'This poll is not bad,' he said, adjusting the wig, 'but it needs something more.'

So we borrowed a velvet bandeau with brown ostrich

feathers from Lady Catherine. She has three bandeaux she makes Anne wear, but Anne hates them.

'You are a perfect queen,' said Denny, clapping Chamberlayne on the back.

I thought he was right. Chamberlayne did look very grand, especially with the tall feathers on his head.

'My dear, you are too kind,' said Chamberlayne, putting his left hand to his throat and fluttering his eyelashes like Lydia does when she is flirting with an officer.

We gave him an ostrich feather fan, and he pouted and posed like a blushing maiden. His arms were smoother than Denny's and his face was softer, and he really did look like a woman.

'Now we will go and talk to Mr. Hurst,' said Denny. 'Only this time, Chamberlayne will speak to him alone and we will watch. Take care Lady Catherine does not see you, Chamberlayne.'

'Lady Catherine is very near-sighted,' I said.

'So much the better,' said Denny. 'Though I think her clothes look better on Chamberlayne than on her!'

So we went again to the Assembly Rooms. Denny and I sat just inside the door of the gaming-room, and Chamberlayne waited outside until Mr. Hurst came out. He drank a great deal of wine, so he often left the gaming-table to go somewhere private. When he was returning, Chamberlayne met him at the door and smiled at him, simpering and fanning himself. Mr. Hurst smiled back.

'Allow me,' he said, holding the door open.

'Oh no, thank you, sir,' said Chamberlayne in a high girl's voice. 'I am waiting for my friend.'

I thought I should have died for trying not to laugh.

'Is she as pretty as you?' asked Mr. Hurst. He thought he was not observed, but Denny and I could see and hear him perfectly.

Chamberlayne just smiled and giggled, shrugging his shoulders and waving the fan in his right hand.

'You are a d*** fine girl,' said Mr. Hurst, nodding at Chamberlayne and going in to take his seat at the table.

Denny and I joined him, and we had a game of loo, only Anne kept winning and we were out very quickly. When we arrived in Bath, I thought Anne was very dull, but now I think she is very quick. I am sure if Lady Catherine were my mother, I would want to be good at something and not tell her. She always criticises every one. And I think Mr. Stephens likes Anne. I tried to flirt with him, but he was not interested, even when I wore Rigge's Liquid Bloom.

When Mr. Hurst was out of the game, he left the room again, and Chamberlayne was still by the door and we could see them talking to each other.

Well, and we had a very good evening, and we met Chamberlayne later when he had changed back into his soldier's uniform. He said Mr. Hurst was very complimentary and tried to kiss him on the cheek when they said goodbye at the Assembly Rooms, only Chamberlayne dodged him.

The next night, Chamberlayne put the same clothes on, and he and Mr. Hurst had several private conversations together, and Mr. Hurst kissed him on the cheek.

'He wants to walk out with me tomorrow when Mrs. Hurst is having tea with a friend,' said Chamberlayne.

So he dressed again in the red velvet robe and ostrich feathers, and he was about to stroll along the Crescent when whom should we see on the other side of the road but Lady Catherine and Anne. Anne was trying to look in a dress shop window and Lady Catherine was pulling her away. I do not understand Lady Catherine. Mamma loves to look in shops, and she often reads *The Mirror of the Graces* with me. It is her favourite book. I think poor Anne is very unlucky. My mother is much more sensible.

I waved hard at Chamberlayne until he noticed me, and he saw Lady Catherine and turned and walked quickly in the other direction. Then Mr. Hurst appeared and he hurried after Chamberlayne. Denny and I followed. Mr. Hurst was so taken up with Chamberlayne that he did not notice us. I thought it must be nice to have a man so interested in you. I was with Denny, but he does not seem to like girls, only as friends.

In the distance, I saw Mr. Hurst look around him to make sure Mrs. Hurst was not there, and then he took Chamberlayne's hand and kissed it. Then he took a ring from his pocket and slipped it onto Chamberlayne's finger before hurrying away.

'He wants to meet me again tomorrow,' said Chamberlayne, when we caught up with him. 'He says I am a beautiful woman and he wants to install me in a house of my own and visit me every day.'

How we laughed. And so Lydia is not the only one who makes a joke. This idea was all mine and Denny's. I could not wait to tell her.

The next day, I was walking with Jane and Charles, and just as we passed the inn that Denny said was a Molly House, out came Denny and Chamberlayne. They looked very merry and they could hardly talk for laughing.

'Come round this corner with us and watch the door of the inn,' said Denny.

So we stood around the corner and waited. Two tall women with ostrich feathers and big stampers went in.

'Look at that shap,' said Chamberlayne, pointing to one lady's extravagant hat.

I do not know different languages, so I asked what language this was, and they said 'Parlyaree', so I think perhaps it was French.

We waited some more, and then the door opened and a stout man with a red face came out, looking around him very secretively. You will be astonished when I tell you it was Mr. Hurst. He did not see us, but we knew it was him.

'The hypocrite,' said Denny. 'Do you still want to marry him, Chamberlayne?'

I did not see why Mr. Hurst was a hypocrite for going into an inn, but I knew Chamberlayne could not marry him in any case, because Mr. Hurst was already married, and anyway, Chamberlayne is a man.

'Oh no,' said Chamberlayne. 'But we will have our sport with him and he will know he cannot insult my friend.'

He and Denny linked arms and walked on with us as we took a turn about the Crescent.

The following day, Chamberlayne dressed in the red robe and met Mr. Hurst again, and I watched with Denny. Mr. Hurst was very happy to see Chamberlayne. This time he gave our friend a necklace. They were talking together very close when all of a sudden we heard a bellow from across the street. It was Lady Catherine.

'That is my dress!' she shouted. 'I insist you return it.'

Anne and Miss Bishop were with her, and they made faces that said they were sorry, but they could not stop her.

Chamberlayne looked at her coolly and waved the fan in front of his face. 'I think you are mistaken, madam,' he said, in a high voice.

'I am not mistaken,' said Lady Catherine. 'I may be near-sighted, but I know that is my dress. I had my own sempstress make it before we came to Bath.'

Then she went right up to Chamberlayne and looked at him closely. 'Who are you, miss? I have not seen you before. You are very bold with your assertions.'

Chamberlayne pouted and shrugged his shoulders. 'My name is Nelly, madam.'

'Well, Miss Nelly, you should be ashamed of yourself. Give me the bandeau now and come with me to return the dress. Then I will notify an officer that you have stolen it from me.'

And she snatched the ostrich feather bandeau from his head. Unfortunately, the wig came with it, and underneath we could all see Chamberlayne's short hair.

Mr. Hurst spluttered. 'What what what!' he said. 'Are you a man?'

Chamberlayne knew the game was over. 'Yes,' he said. 'I am.'

'Disgraceful!' said Mr. Hurst. 'I will fetch an officer too.'

'Why will you do that?' asked Denny. 'Are you prejudiced against Chamberlayne? Do you want to take the officer to the Molly House with you?'

'I do not know what you mean,' said Mr. Hurst, his face even redder than before.

'We saw you there,' said Chamberlayne, in his normal voice.

'You saw him in a Molly House?' We all turned to Lady Catherine. 'What was he doing there?'

'Making a bargain,' said Chamberlayne.

'Indeed,' said Lady Catherine. 'And did you wear my dress there, sir?'

'I did not,' said Chamberlayne. 'I only wore it to talk to Mr. Hurst.'

Lady Catherine's eyes were sparkling. She looked uncommonly amused. I had never seen her like that before.

'Indeed,' said Lady Catherine again. 'So you admit it is my dress?'

'We only borrowed it, mamma,' began Anne.

But Lady Catherine interrupted her. 'Be quiet, Anne. I must say, I think you look very fetching in my dress, sir. Does he not?' And she turned to Denny.

'He does, Lady Catherine,' stammered Denny, all astonishment.

'Then we shall say no more about the matter,' said Lady Catherine. 'You will go to my rooms with Miss Bishop. I trust you have clothes of your own there?'

'Indeed I do,' said Chamberlayne. 'Your ladyship is very kind.'

'And you and Mr. Denny will stay and take tea with me,'

said Lady Catherine. 'I have long wondered what happens inside a Molly House. As for you, sir,' she turned to Mr. Hurst, 'you are a disgrace. Return to your wife this instant, or I will fetch an officer and turn you over to him for corrupting this innocent young lady.' And she pointed to Chamberlayne.

Mr. Hurst blew air through his lips hard, like a horse, but he realised he was beaten. And I must say, he deserved a harsher penalty, but he knew we all thought he was very silly, and perhaps that was punishment enough. Lydia will laugh so much when I tell her.

Anne and I became closer friends after that, and she did not marry Mr. Stephens. She seems perfectly happy to wait until she meets another man. I think she is right. I wanted to marry as soon as I could, because Lydia is married, but now I have learned more about men. Some of them, like Mr. Hurst, are not kind and do not treat their wives well; and some of them, like Denny and Chamberlayne, do not like to marry women. I do not understand that, but I know it is so and I am happy for them. Maybe they will take me to a Molly House one day. I confess it would please me very much, for I still do not quite know what it is, but now I think the tall women with big stampers are not women at all, but men. What a surprise!

I almost forgot. Some time ago, I had a letter from my sister Lizzy. She was organising a procession to promote the cause of women's education. I may join her another time. This time I think I learned a lot in Bath.

CHAPTER 9

MR. BENNET – NO COMPASSION FOR MY POOR NERVES

I never set out to be a poisoner. These things come upon us by stealth, and before we know it, we are enmeshed in a life of crime. How I long for the innocent days, when my biggest concern was the state of my wife's nerves, and the most strenuous action I had to perform was to see three of my daughters married.

After Jane and Lizzy left, my life was dull in the extreme, and even Lydia's absence gave me cause for contemplation at how lucky our escape from scandal had been, and at such little cost to us. Only two daughters were left on our hands, and my wife had ample leisure, and a house almost as empty as her head. Herein lay the problem. With even less to occupy her, she turned her attentions to improving the person closest to her—myself. It was scarcely to be borne. Her ceaseless chatter was a constant dripping, and I was completely worn down by it. I could scarce fall asleep at night before she woke me with some trivial tale of outwitting the linen-draper's assistant, or being slighted by the butcher's wife. In the daytime, I spent as much time as I could in managing my estate, but truth to tell, there was little to be done. I am not a fox-chasing man, and I do not care for shooting or gaming. I prefer to keep to my library, but Mrs. Bennet had many little plans for its redecoration, and I was obliged to spend my days discussing wallpaper and carpets and making trips to town to choose the latest fabrics and designs, which we could ill afford.

Then Mrs. Bennet started on a round of visits, befreinding tiresome ladies in neighbouring villages and further afield, and it was on one of these occasions that she became fast freinds with a woman of her own age named Lady Maria. Lady Maria's estate is much grander than Longbourn, and her character is even more indolent than Mrs. Bennet's, but they struck up a freindship founded on the notion of being ill-used by their children and neglected by their husbands. I approved the freindship, because it took Mrs. Bennet away from our home for several days at a time and furnished me some respite from her ceaseless attacks of nerves. When Mrs. Bennet returned, however, her presence was even more irksome, and my mind turned to ever-more fanciful ways of evading her.

My first recourse was to visit my dear daughters Jane and Lizzy, but Mrs. Bennet complained at being left at home on her own and made sure to accompany me. I was mindful there was only so much of her presence that the Bingleys and Darcys were willing to endure, so we did not stay long. Then we made visits to the Gardiners in London, and they were a great comfort, but I did not wish to outstay our welcome, and besides, the young Gardiners were not restful to be with. They had that boisterousness of character that children will have, and the girls were always demanding we look at this handiwork or that doll, while the boys never ceased running around and laughing and throwing things. Mrs. Bennet, as was to be expected, complained constantly at the toll this took on her nerves, and for once I was almost ready to sympathise with her.

I had some respite when we returned to Longbourn, because a great mystery had arisen in regard to Charlotte Collins. No one knew where she was, but she had not been seen at Meryton for many months, and when Mr. Collins visited her parents, he came alone. This state of affairs afforded many opportunities for gossip among the ladies of the village, and speculation as to Charlotte's whereabouts occupied much of Mrs. Bennet's time. Even Lizzy seemed not to know where Mr. Collins's wife was gone. This led me to the natural conclusion that either the stupid fellow had done away with her, or she had finally tired of her husband and left him. And she would have had my hearty support if she had done so.

Unhappily, I could not leave my own wife. We still had two unmarried daughters, and I did not wish to bring dishonour on my family. I did imagine, though, that my wife might be prevailed on to leave me, once Mary and Kitty were married, were I to make a greater effort to be disagreeable. My previous attempts had proved fruitless, but on learning of Charlotte's disappearance, I was not without hope.

Until that happy event, I tried to persuade Mrs. Bennet to set up home with our daughter Lydia, but Lydia and

Wickham were always moving from one house to another, and constantly asking for money, and I foresaw that situation would not long satisfy Mrs. Bennet. I knew Jane and Lizzy would not take her; Mary and Kitty had no homes of their own. Then Lady Maria came to visit.

Lady Maria was a very equitable person, freindly and kind, as long as her own comfort was not disturbed. Alas, I could not say the same of Pug. Wherever Lady Maria went, from parlour to dining-room, he waddled after her on his fat, ungainly legs, his brow wrinkled, his face discontented, emitting a constant barrage of wheezes and snorts, and filling the air with a noxious odour. He was the most unhealthy creature I had ever seen, over-fed and over-indulged by his mistress. He spent much of the day asleep. When told to sit, he would stand, his lolling tongue seeming to mock the command-giver. When Lady Maria ate a sweetmeat, Pug would whine until a cake or biscuit were produced for him. His mistress told us his constitution was delicate, and apart from the food on Lady Maria's plate, he would eat only a little boiled chicken or calf's liver, and drink only milk.

It struck me more than once that Pug had many similarities with Mrs. Bennet. She too was fond of sweet things. Her preoccupation with her nerves led her to spend more and more time in bed, which I welcomed, until the ringing of her bell and insistence on my presence disturbed me so frequently that I took to spending many hours in the potting shed, even though it was unheated and most unpleasant in winter. Moreover, her hours without exercise were causing her girth to increase and her legs to lose their strength. Her brow was increasingly wrinkled, and when she did attempt to walk any distance she was starting to wheeze. It wanted only a few snorts and a lolling tongue for her to become indistinguishable from Lady Maria's lap-dog.

This state of affairs was becoming unbearable. I could not escape, but I could not remain without my own nerves being torn to shreds. And then, one day, I saw Pug alone in the garden. This was most unusual, but Lady Maria and my wife were deep in confabulation in the parlour, no doubt fussing over the price of lace and Charlotte Lucas's absence, and Pug had wandered out when the maid was occupied in serving tea to her mistress. I observed from a distance. Pug was not used to freedom. He sniffed the grass and chased a sparrow. He buried his nose in a cluster of daisies and sneezed. He became braver, and gambolled up and down the lawn, stopping frequently to toy with a snail or paw the gravel walk. For once, he was behaving like a real dog, and I became more sympathetic towards him. Then he approached the flower-beds, and before I could stop him, he went straight to a patch of foxglove and licked the poisonous purple flowers. I ran at once to rescue him, and was able to extract him before he had eaten any thing, as far as I could ascertain.

For the rest of the day, I observed Pug closely. Lady Maria was unaware of his excursion. Pug drooled a little more than usual, and it was less *pleasant* to be in his vicinity, the air around him being even less sweet than before, but other than that, he was none the worse for his little adventure. The episode had given me an idea, however. My wife frequently took a little decoction of foxglove for her headaches. The effect of a larger dose might prove disastrous. A larger dose such as might be administered by mistake, if some one added their own distillation of foxglove to her regular medicine, but whose provenance would not be detected, since she already had the draught at her disposal and the amount in the bottle would not be significantly less. And might not Pug prove a ready patient to try the cure until it was perfected? An amount of foxglove sufficient to fell that fat little creature would surely prove equally fatal to a human.

I do not say I devised this scheme lightly. I was at my very wits' end, and unable to think of any other recourse. I would go so far as to say I was even a little unhinged at the time, with countless calls on my mental resources from women and pugs and Lord knows what else. A lesser man might have taken to drink. I took to poison.

After a careful search among the books in my library, I found Culpeper's *Complete Herbal* and two other volumes that provided instruction in how to prepare a decoction of foxglove. At nightfall, when all had retired, I crept into the garden and gathered a handful of foxglove leaves and stems. I left them in my potting shed and was returning to the house when I heard a short, sharp bark. Pug had entered the garden for an evening constitutional. Since his last excursion, Lady Maria had taken to allowing him to wander at will, prevailing on Mrs. Bennet to have the kitchen door left open so he could come and go as he fancied. I was astonished my wife permitted this, given that she is prone to beleive every noise in the night to be an evil-doer come to murder us in our beds, but such were Lady Maria's powers of persuasion.

I reached down and patted Pug, and he licked my hand and trotted along at my heels. This would not do. I was beginning to feel some affection for the little creature. I therefore endeavoured to shake him off and told him to shoo, but he would not leave my side as I went into the kitchen, filled a jug with water and took it to the potting shed. Then I closed the shed door and returned to the house, ready to pursue my plan on the morrow.

The next day, I had little chance to advance my strategy, for I was kept busy by my remaining unwed daughters. Mary had a new music teacher who was almost as silly as herself, but whom Mrs. Bennet was determined I must meet, and I allowed that music lessons would at least occupy Mary's time profitably. Mary had spent many hours repining at her ill luck in Mr. Collins marrying Charlotte Lucas, and when that young lady fell in the river during a picnic with Mary and Kitty on Charlotte's last visit, I half suspected Mary's involvement in the affair. Since then, however, Mary had kept silent on the subject of the Collinses, and I imagined she had accepted she was unlikely ever to see the inside of the Rosings parsonage or become more intimate with its incumbent. She continued to play peices that were ever increasing in their dramatic quality, and when she was practising Bach's Toccata and Fugue on a stormy night, I almost expected the door to fly open and a half-crazed character in a long cloak and dark hat to burst through and demand my money or my wife. (There. I too am becoming obsessed. I should say, my money or my life. I am afraid I should have had no hesitation in fulfilling the former request. It is only the law that regards Mrs. Bennet as my property. For myself, I would happily forego that possession.) Mary was now diligently practising the work of Beethoven, particularly his sonatas for the pianoforte, and rejoiced in the more tempestuous movements. She did not always play accurately, but there were many notes on the page, and I dare say she tried to use most of them. The effect was certainly arresting, and her new teacher was full of praise, as well he might be, when it seemed likely her want of talent would prolong his teaching career, and consequent income, indefinitely.

Kitty had lately returned from a visit to Bath, and could not be restrained from telling us without cease of an episode she had witnessed at the gaming-tables. Her mother and Lady Maria made her repeat the details many times, with so many exclamations and trivial questions as to the attire and accoutrements of the principal players that had nothing to do with the substance of the story, that I could not help but suspect Kitty was concealing a greater misdeed of her own by distracting us with this other narrative. But I let it pass. If she has learned some skills, even if only in the art of diverting her mother's attention, it at least indicates she is taking some initiative at last. I have hopes she may follow in her sister Elizabeth's footsteps and claim the rights of women to a solid education. My daughters think I am unaware of this adventure and resulting court case, but I am immensely proud of her.

Kitty's stories served to fill my day, and it was not until late afternoon that I was able to repair to the potting shed with a tea-pot of near boiling water abstracted from the kitchen when the housekeeper was occupied in serving the ladies. I had no means of a fire, but I plunged the foxglove leaves into the pot of hot water and left them to steep. Pug accompanied me, a frown on his face, and I swore him to secrecy. He only barked.

The next morning, I returned to the shed and added some sugar to the mixture to make it more palatable. I had intended to try the medicine on Pug, to test its strength, but I was becoming fond of the ugly little creature and could not bring myself to feed it to him. I took a small taste of the draught and found it bitter, so I added more sugar. This at least made it a little more drinkable, though any one taking it in quantities sufficient to have the desired effect would have had to swallow the pot in one draught. I left the tea-pot on the bench and returned to the house, where I spent an interminable evening listening to the ladies' discussions of the latest fashions, and Mary's discourses on what she termed "storm and drang". My head was spinning, and I was beginning to think the best way out might be for me to drink the foxglove mixture myself.

I was too discouraged to visit the potting shed that night, but we were awoken in the small hours by Pug's insistent yapping and the sound of retching in the garden.

'Mr. Bennet! Mr. Bennet!' screamed my wife. 'We shall all be murdered in our beds. Go and see what is happening. No, do not go. He may have a knife. Save Pug. No, do not leave the house.'

I put my coat on and hastened to the back door. There, on the grass, was a scoundrel on his hands and knees, my pruning knife on the floor beside him, his body being purged both upwards and downwards. Pug was wading in the foul mess around the man, barking incessantly. The moon illuminated the scene, and I saw at a glance that the potting shed door was open and the tea-pot with the decoction lay on its side. It was plain to see what had happened. The man had broken into the shed and picked up the knife prior to breaking into our house. Overcome with thirst, he had drunk from the tea-pot, and the strong decoction was now having its wonted effect.

'Save me, sir, save me,' he choked.

I sent one of the servants to fetch the apothecary, and we dragged the sick man to a cleaner spot on the grass, where our cook administered warm water and brandy. Mrs. Bennet and Lady Maria joined us, chattering in nervous excitement. In the confusion, I went quietly to the shed and removed all traces of the tea-pot and its deadly liquid. Then I returned to the fellow as he lay groaning on the grass, partially recovered. It was vital he tell no one about my essays in brewing poisonous plants. Allowing the mixture to be discovered had been my first mistake.

'I do not know what you were doing in my shed,' I said, 'but I am willing to overlook it this once, on condition you do not return.'

'Mr. Bennet!' exclaimed my wife. 'Are you mad? He has a knife! He will murder us all. We should take him to the cells. Should we not take him to the cells, Lady Maria? Indeed, we should call the constable. My poor nerves. I have such a headache. You cannot imagine.'

The man groaned and looked at Mrs. Bennet and then at me, with what might even be said to pass for a glimmer of understanding.

'And I do not know what strange kinds of tea you keep in your shed, sir, but I am willing to overlook it too. Some things are best kept secret, ain't they?' And I will swear he winked at me, or tried to wink, but was overcome by another fit of vomiting. Pug remained at my side, barking and snuffling, and I felt fit to vomit too, at the thought of the crime I had been ready to commit.

The man was removed to the stables and was recovered sufficiently by the next morning to leave, with a firm avowal that he would not return. Pug was praised for his action in saving the household, and Lady Maria made ready to depart. The exhilaration had proved too much for her indolent nature. I was glad to see her go.

My own nerves were now in tatters, and so were those of my wife, though it may be imagined how much her own nerves took precedence. She consoled me, however, with Lady Maria's parting promise, in which I learned of my next two mistakes. First, Pug was a bitch, and secondly, because we had so appreciated her role in saving our household, next time she had a litter we would be given not one, but three puppies.

The wild thought came to my disordered brain that this new trial was more than I could bear. To have one pug was misfortune enough, but to allow three in the house was worse than carelessness. How would I cope with the snorting and the wheezing, the slobbering and the hair shedding?

It was not long, however, before an even greater trial came upon me. A week after the incident with the burglar in the garden, I was surprised to see the same fellow lurking near the potting shed one evening. He beckoned me over and indicated we should take a seat inside. I thought I should enquire after his health, and he assured me he was quite recovered, and asked after my own health and then, more surprisingly, after my wife's well-being. As he said this, he winked at me several times.

'Not made her some more of that tea, 'ave yer?' he asked, grinning all over his ugly face.

'I do not know what you are talking about,' I said. 'That potion was intended for the dog. Pug was ailing, and I was told that foxglove is very efficacious for purging the body.'

'Laws, it purged me, right enough,' he said, wheezing and grunting like an old goat. 'Now, 'ere's the thing. If you was to have some more of that stuff, I knows a few chaps what would be interested, like. It's got to be strong, mind. Stronger than purging. What you did, it got me to thinking, see. If some one wants to poison another party, and I'm not saying as they does, mind, but if they does, then this 'ere's a good way. You give 'em the same as what the apothecary gives 'em, but stronger. The person dies. Surgeon opens 'em up. From what my pal at the Old Bailey tells me, there ain't no proof left inside with a poison like this. Just the heart stops working. Surgeon knows they're taking foxglove, thinks they've had a overreaction, and there you are.'

He leered at me unpleasantly. I was most indignant.

'I could not possibly be party to such a thing,' I said. 'That is murder.'

'You was party to it before, wasn't you?' said the scoundrel. 'I didn't tell no one, but I might see my ways to telling 'em, mightn't I, if you don't help with this little business what I'm proposing.'

'You have no proof whatever that that was my intention,' I expostulated.

'Come come, sir. We 'ave all the proof we need, and we can always make up some more, me and my pals.'

I could see I would be easily outwitted, and then what should I do?

'Who would be your clients for this little service of mine?' I enquired.

'Men like you, with wives what talk too much.'

He could see I was wavering. I did feel sympathy for any one in my situation.

'Give me a few months to perfect the decoction,' I said, 'and I will see what I can supply.'

⁓

Some time later, our household was extended by the arrival of three small pugs. Mrs. Bennet, who had anxiously awaited their arrival, was overjoyed to see them, but revolted by the mess they made, and was quick to leave their training to Kitty, who was in raptures over these tiny creatures. When Kitty was not playing with them, they followed me around the garden, digging holes in the flower-beds and around the apricot trees, and I had to be constantly alert to ensure they did not partake of the more dangerous plants and berries. It was very distressing and put a lot of pressure on my nerves, busy as I was preparing for my unwanted visitor, who might appear at any time.

Sure enough, when the pugs had been with us for several weeks, and seemed well on the way to reaching Australia, so big were the holes they were creating in the garden, my unwelcome guest arrived late one evening when I was taking my final constitutional, and once again indicated I should talk to him in the potting shed. His first action was to ask if I wanted to keep the pugs, for, said he, he knew of several homes where good money would be paid for them, no questions asked. I declined, as I had become accustomed to their presence and was even becoming quite fond of them myself. He shrugged and produced some empty bottles.

'Remember why I'm 'ere?' he asked, leering, as was his wont. 'I don't want to 'ave to tell the authorities what you was doing, do I?'

'Indeed not,' I said. I took his bottles and filled them with the draught which, I assured him, I had brewed since his last visit. Then I took another bottle from a shelf and poured us each a large glass.

'Will you join me in toasting our new enterprise, sir?' I asked.

'Not foxglove this, is it?' he asked, winking.

'Indeed not,' I replied indignantly. 'The foxglove decoction is colourless, as you can see. This is elderberry wine. A much more pleasant drink.'

He sniffed it suspiciously, then tossed it down his throat while I continued to toy with the glass in my hand, taking care that not a drop passed my lips. 'Not 'alf bad,' he said. 'Sweet. Tastes of almonds . . .'

I buried his body in the hole the pugs had dug, under the apricot tree whose kernels had furnished the cyanide for the lethal draught. Then I emptied the bottle of mingled cyanide and belladonna poison over the earth, together with the water from the bottles I had passed off as decoction of foxglove, and planted more nightshade over the grave for good measure.

My only hope is that the pugs will continue to dig elsewhere and will be sufficiently distracted to leave his remains in peace. It is a constant vigil and my head aches terribly, but my wife cannot persuade me to take any medicine to counteract my frequent migraines. Knowing I am immovable in this respect, she has returned to cataloguing her own misfortunes and ailments. What with her never-ending complaints, Mary's tempestuous playing of the pianoforte, and the pugs' snorting and snuffling all night outside our bedroom door, I am quite worn down by the weight of it all.

No one has any compassion for my poor nerves.

CHAPTER 10

LYDIA WICKHAM – DAYLIGHT ROBBERY

Lord, what a joke! I can hardly lift my pen for laughing. I never supposed I, Lydia Wickham, should be a writer. But life surprises us all. And I always wanted to live comfortably in London, but I never dreamed I should, after I married Wickham and found he had no money, so that is another surprise.

Wickham and me moved house so often when we married, we did not have a home to call our own, and we spent much time with our friends and family. Mr. Darcy would not allow Wickham to visit Pemberley, which I thought was very mean-spirited of him, considering all Wickham did for him when he was a boy. But I did go and visit Lizzy on my own, and Jane and Bingley often welcomed us both, and they are only in the next county. Papa would not permit Kitty to come and stay with me, but I saw her sometimes in Bath. My sister Mary I did not wish to see. She is so tiresome. Only think, I gave her my old bonnet one time I was at Longbourn, and later I asked if I might not have it back, if she did not wish to wear it, and she said she had thrown it away because it was badly trimmed. And I only changed the trim twice and it looked as good as new, and would have done very nicely for her, as she never travels beyond Meryton. Papa was still cool with me, though that was of no consequence. When was he ever concerned about my welfare? He did not even attend my wedding! And though mamma was always glad to see me, I found it very dull to be at Longbourn now the soldiers were gone.

After one short visit to my parents, I met Wickham at an inn in London. He was come down from York, and I was going on to visit my friend Harriet Forster at Brighton. I meant to treat her, but Wickham said he had no money to spare for me. However, as he and I were walking down the road near the inn the night before my departure, we saw a man stumbling unsteadily, evidently in liquor. He was weaving around the road with his greatcoat under his arm and a canvas purse in his breeches pocket. And then, two women ran past and pushed him, and he was so drunk he fell over. He called out, but they ran off, taking his coat and purse with them. We pursued them a short distance, but they dropped the things and turned into a side alley, where they disappeared up some stairs. Well, the man was still in the street, and no one was near us, so Wickham picked up the purse and coat, and I am sure he meant to return them to the man, but when we went back to the street, he was gone.

The purse had four half-crowns and thirty sovereigns in it, but the greatcoat had nothing. Wickham said the man was not there, and we found the money in the street, so we should divide it between us. Gracious, what a lark! Now I had money when I went to Brighton in the stage-coach the next day. Wickham stayed in London on business, and we said we would meet back in York, because he did not know how long his affairs would take.

Colonel Forster was distant towards me, and hardly asked how Wickham was, but Harriet and I are very thick, and we spent so much time discussing the latest fashions and planning balls that I scarce knew where the days went. Every evening we had dances and dinners with the officers, and I was every one's favourite. I wished Wickham could see me. He was sometimes a little forgetful that I was the main person in his life, and it would not have hurt him to see how I was favoured by other men. He was no longer an officer himself, but he could not be insensitive to their regard for me.

When I was ready to leave Brighton, Lizzy sent me a letter inviting me to go to Cambridge. I thought it was as good a plan as any, as it is not far from the Great North Road, which I had to take to reach York.

Colonel Forster wished me a safe trip and urged me to be careful because there was a dangerous highwayman at large. He then narrated the story of the drunk man with the greatcoat and the purse. This man had gone to the watch-house, and a woman was arrested, but she said it could not be her, because the drunk man said the woman had run away and she said she could not run because she was lame, and they brought in a surgeon who said this was true, her joints were swollen and she could not move quickly. So they found that the man was in liquor and had lost his purse through carelessness, and the woman was fined sixpence and discharged. I was relieved at this verdict, because I did not want her to be arrested, but if she was lame, then she was in no danger anyway, so that was all right. And he had no call to be so drunk. I do not know how he even managed to stay upright. He quite brought the affair on himself.

Colonel Forster was very pressing in his warning, and I said, if things are so bad, I will borrow a horse and ride to York more quickly than if I went in the stage-coach, which might be a target for robbers. He was very unwilling, but I had him harness a mare, a dark creature called Black Bess, and I shewed him I could ride very well, even though I had to ride side-saddle. He was grudging in his admiration, but he acknowledged I rode as well as any man. I asked if I might keep the horse and sell it and return the money to him at a later date, so the journey would cost me only four guineas, which was the price of the horse, instead of twelve guineas, which was the price of a stage-coach ticket from London to York. Was not that a good plan?

I said goodbye to Harriet and set off for London, accompanied by my old friend Denny, who was stationed in Brighton. Lord, how he laughed when I told him I wanted a man's saddle so I could ride comfortably the rest of my way home. And he lent me his spare pair of breeches and gave me a wide-brimmed hat and a cloak. I pulled the breeches on over my muslin gown and covered my body and face with the cloak and hat. Only think what fun!

When I reached London, Denny bought me some jockey-boots, which came halfway up my legs, because my little shoes did not look right with the breeches. Then he exchanged my side-saddle for a gentleman's saddle, which he put on Black Bess. He went on to Bath and I continued to Smithfield-market at the start of the Great North Road. I took some refreshment, but I did not want to be noticed in my man's clothes, so I removed my breeches and boots and spent the night at an inn.

The next day, I donned my man's clothes and boots once more and rode forth. Now I was on a horse and not in a coach, I took more notice of my surroundings, and I rode quickly to avoid the ragamuffins who were clustered around Islington-green. As I trotted past, I observed a warehouse with the notice "Gentlemen with Nails in their Boots not Admitted", and a shop proclaiming it as "The New Paradise". How I did laugh!

Holloway-road was well named, being sunken and muddy and very hollow. I had not taken notice before, because I was always so excited to reach London, and in any case, I usually approached London from Longbourn, and that road was different. Now I thought this was the dullest road I had ever seen. Highgate-hill gave me some respite, and when I reached the top I heard the sound of what I supposed were the Bow Bells and stopped to listen, but I did not turn back like Dick Whittington. I had no wish to become Mayor of London. Lord, how dull that sounds. Only, I would have changed the laws so that lace was cheap and balls were held every night of the week, so perhaps it was not such a bad idea.

I continued to ride, and thought I would dine at the Swan Inn in Bell-bar before continuing my journey to Cambridge, but as I approached, I saw a stage-coach stopped beside the road, and all the women in a great flutter, and the men storming and cursing. I would have ridden past, but the driver waved at me and I slowed down, though I did not dismount, for I did not want any one to see me at close quarters.

'Take heed,' he said. 'There is a highwayman in these parts. He has just now tried to rob us of our money. It was only our blunderbuss that drove him away empty-handed. Will you go on, sir, and alert the constable at the next town?'

I nodded, though you can imagine how I felt, being a woman riding on my own. Only, I thought it would be exciting to meet a real highwayman, so I was in two minds.

'He was a very handsome fellow, from what we could see,' said one of the ladies. The other women joined in. 'He wore ruffles and lace and was very well dressed.' 'Handsome. Like a cavalier.' 'Dark hair under his mask. Tall. Handsome.'

As I rode on, I thought I should not mind meeting this particular highwayman, but it might be as well to get to Cambridge as fast as I could. I would sleep somewhere on the way, so as not to be travelling in the dark, and reach my destination on the morrow. I therefore did not have lunch at the Swan, but I bought a Stilton cheese and a pork pie and ate them by the roadside outside the village, and they served well enough.

As I was eating, a Scotsman on horseback approached me. I touched my hat to him, and he stopped to exchange news of the road. At this, Black Bess became very friendly with his gelding, and edged up to him, as though to prevent them proceeding. The Scotsman became very alarmed and at once handed me his purse and entreated me not to shoot him. I perceived he had taken me for a highwayman, and I could hardly mount my horse for laughing as he cantered away to London.

This got me to thinking. If I could make money only by being mistook for a highwayman, without the fuss of a gun or a blunderbuss, I should do very well. I hoped I would meet another traveller and see how this plan might develop.

I proceeded another hour, and it was wearisome work in the saddle. I was minded to sell my horse at the next town and take the stage-coach instead. I had a little money, and with what I would get for the horse I would be able to buy an inside seat in a coach without the fag of riding. I still had my woman's clothes, and I would dispose of the breeches and boots somehow. These and other thoughts occupied me until the sun started to set and a lone figure appeared in the distance. I was not greatly disturbed, and I was minded to try my luck one last time and see if the other horseman could be persuaded to part with his money.

The sun sunk further, and the road around me was now quite hard to distinguish. The trees cast long shadows and I did not feel quite so merry, but I consoled myself that this would be a fine story to tell Wickham. The other horseman was advancing at a trot, and I could see now that he was tall and wore a greatcoat with ruffles at the neck and lace on the cuffs that protruded from his sleeves, and his face was hidden behind a mask. I refused to be frightened, however, and I pulled my hat down further over my face and tucked one hand in my cloak, as though to conceal a pistol.

The stranger's horse cantered up to me, and the man raised his gun in the air and brandished it. We spoke not a word. But my horse began to play her old tricks, and nosed up to his black stallion as though to push him off the road. The rider kicked at Bess, but she was not to be deterred.

Then he fired a shot into the air, and she reared up in fright, throwing me to the ground. My cloak fell to the side, and though my face was still covered, it was evident, from the set of my shoulders and the softness of my form under my muslin gown, that I was not of the male sex.

At this, the rider was all solicitation. He jumped from his horse and offered me his hand.

'Pray, do not be concerned,' he said. 'I will not harm you. But I am afraid you are already hurt. Is there any thing I can do for you?'

I shook my head. I did not know whether to laugh or be angry, so I remained silent.

'Allow me to help you up,' he continued. 'I have some liquor in this bottle that will restore your spirits. Let us drink a little together and then I will take you to an inn. We can perhaps spend the night there in comfort, and if we share a room, we can defray our expenses.'

He put his arm around me, and I felt his touch around my waist and his fingers moving higher, before he let out an almighty roar.

'What the d***!' he exclaimed, as my knee met him in his tenderest parts.

'What indeed!' I answered. 'Will you use a woman in this way?'

He let go my arm and stared at me in great astonishment. 'Lydia!'

I pulled Wickham's mask from his face. 'Is this the way you treat a woman?' I asked. 'And what of your wife? What would she have said? You did not know the woman on the ground was I, your loving companion.'

It wanted only a moment before he regained his composure.

'My wife would have said it was the very greatest joke I ever played on her,' he replied. 'Come now, let us be friends. I knew who you were as soon as I saw you.'

'As soon as you saw under my cloak, you mean,' I replied with spirit.

He pulled off my hat and ruffled my hair. 'I have a very particular interest in what is under your cloak,' he said. 'And a very particular interest in taking you to an inn to examine your injuries.'

At the thought of somewhere to lie down and sleep, a violent yawn escaped me. 'Lord, I am tired!' I admitted.

'Then we shall ride on to the nearest inn and stay the night,' he said.

'Will not the constables recognise you?' I asked. 'The ladies I spoke to before Bell Bar gave a good description of your person.'

'How did they describe me?' he asked.

'Tall, dark and handsome.'

He burst out laughing. 'And what do you say?' he asked.

But I declined to answer.

'It is true,' he said, 'that I need to dispose of this greatcoat. Will you give me your cloak and hat? Surely you can have no need of them now. And you will have no need of any clothes tonight.'

I was still very vexed with him, but I did not want him to be arrested. I had not paid heed before to the penalty for being a highwayman, but now I recognised it as a hanging matter. It was well I had not been apprehended myself. So I gave him my cloak and hat, and he threw the greatcoat and ruffles in the ditch. Then we rode on to Welwyn and stayed the night at the White Hart. While dinner was being prepared, I spoke to the innkeeper's wife, a trollopy-looking woman who regarded me suspiciously, but, when she heard my story, that I was a wronged wife returning home with my wayward husband, she was happy to enter into the spirit of the game. What a lark! She slipped a draught into Wickham's drink before we repaired to our room, and he spent the night in a stupor in the armchair while I slept soundly in the bed.

In the morning, while Wickham was still asleep, the innkeeper's wife woke me early with a new cloak and hat, which I donned over my breeches and boots. Then I went down to the dining-room and ate some rolls and drank some coffee.

'I have no money for the room, but he will pay,' I said, pointing up the stairs.

'Indeed he will, ma'am,' she said, laughing. 'I have another draught for him here, and this one'll give him a good purging. He won't be trying his tricks again, not for a long time!'

Well, and so I never got to Cambridge. Instead, I went back with Black Bess the way I was come, and when I got to London I sold her for four guineas and took the post to Longbourn. I did not know quite what I should do there, but I was tired of being a highwayman and fearful I should be discovered. My parents' house is dull in the extreme, but I felt I would be safer in the country, and as Kitty was now away from home, my father had no objection to my visiting.

Alas, while I was gone, my parents had expanded their household. Before I left to stay with the Forsters, mamma talked much about a lady who visited her with a lap-dog, and how this lady would send her a litter of puppies. Now there were three small pugs roaming the house, sniffing in my apartment, leaving reminders of their presence on every rug and carpet. It felt as though my room were no longer mine.

Before I went to bed, I closed the door firmly and looked idly on my bookshelves for something with which to pass the time. I did not enjoy reading, but my nerves were quite unsettled after my exertions and I wanted something to distract me. I traced my finger along the shelves and came across a book positioned a little behind the others, wrapped hastily in brown paper. This caught my attention, and I tore off the wrapper and looked at the volume. It was one I did not recognise: *Fanny Hill, or Memoirs of a Woman of Pleasure* by a Mr. Cleland.

What a joke! That book was a manual of familiar and unfamiliar practices, and I scarce slept a wink all night, so enthralled was I by my discovery.

In the morning, though I could hardly rouse myself for breakfast after my late night, I was called to my father's library and given a stern warning about my conduct. I thought at first papa had discovered Mr. Cleland's book on my shelves, but he made no mention of it. Instead, he alluded to the drunk man in London who had dropped his purse. My Uncle Gardiner had come to hear of the tale, and after talking to the keeper of the inn where we stayed, he surmised that Wickham had taken the man's purse and greatcoat, and that Wickham had then tried to rob a stage-coach. I do not know why my uncle supposed this, and I told papa he was much mistaken, but my father was not to be moved.

'I do not know where Wickham is, Lydia, and I care even less. You are well rid of him, and you will stay here until you have learned some sense,' said he. 'And you will earn your keep. Your mother has three pugs now, and they require exercise and cleaning and Lord knows what else. It is more than my nerves can stand.'

'Then Mrs. Hill can do it,' I said. 'Or Kitty or Mary.'

'Mrs. Hill has other tasks, Kitty did her share before she left to visit Jane, and Mary is occupied with her music,' he said. 'You will do as you are told this once, or your Mr. Wickham will be exposed.'

Well, and so I had to stay. I had no place else to go. I could not warn Wickham, as I did not know his direction, but I was sure he would contact me.

Time passed, and still I did not hear from Wickham. I was heartily sick of the pugs, but I continued to keep them clean, and when another litter joined them, I thought I should scream. They milled around the garden with their ugly little faces, and dug constantly in the flower-beds, only my father would not allow them near the apricot tree. It was his Moor Park, and was his special tree, he said, and he had the gardener put a fence around it. For the rest, the dogs went everywhere, and I followed with a bucket and a little shovel. It was not fit work for a lady.

My only respite was in reading *Fanny Hill*, and after some time I thought, why should only a man write a book such as this? I have as good an imagination as any, and I am sure I can earn money by writing and selling my own stories.

I set to with a will, and my parents and Mary were astonished that I spent every minute when the pugs were asleep engaged in writing. I told them I was writing a journal, and papa said he was pleased I was at last using my time profitably, though he could not imagine what I found to write about that was so interesting, since nothing of note ever happened at Longbourn.

At last my book was finished. I called it *The Alpha of Venus, or Adventures of a Lady Highwayman*, and though I would have published it under a woman's name, I had to use a man's. And so I chose the name Dirk Tippin.

My book was an instant success. My publisher in London told me it was the talk of the inns and clubs, and many ladies had also purchased copies, though they did so secretly. At last I had an income of my own and could buy as many gowns as I wanted. I found, however, that I did not long for dresses and bonnets and balls as I had before. My new work as a writer brought me more self-respect and kept me vastly entertained, even without Mr. Wickham's company.

I bought myself a place in London, and with papa's permission, I moved away from Longbourn and the drudgery of the pugs. He and mamma kept three of them and sold the rest. They both said this was better for their nerves. For myself, I hope never to see a pug again. No more do I want to see Wickham. I am sure now he would have robbed me on the road, had he not recognised me. I heard more stories of highwaymen, but I did not know if they related to him.

The gentleman himself never came to my house and we never spoke to each other again.

One time, though, I was in Hatchards bookshop in Piccadilly, and I heard his voice. I was wearing a wide-brimmed bonnet, and he did not notice me. Lord, it is the last place he would expect to find me. How I laughed when I heard him talking to the shopkeeper.

'I have been away from the city for some time. Do you have the book every one is talking about? It is called *The Alpha of Venus*.'

'Indeed we do, sir. There is a very pleasing leather-bound edition here. Or a small blue calf-skin volume, should you prefer something more discreet.'

'How much do they cost?'

'The leather-bound copy is twelve shillings, and the calf-skin is fifteen shillings and sixpence.'

'Fifteen shillings and sixpence!' he exclaimed. 'That is daylight robbery!'

Well, my dear, and you should know, I thought.

I hid my face, and as I left the shop, my parasol happened to dislodge a pile of books on the table next to Wickham. *Moll Flanders* caught him on the left foot, and several volumes by A Lady landed on his right.

'What the d***!' he exclaimed.

But I sailed past and stepped out onto the street. I thought I should have died for laughing!

CHAPTER 11

CHARLOTTE COLLINS – A TRUE ROMANTIC

Penrith, Australia, July 5, 18**

My dear Eliza,

It is some years since your wedding, and my thoughts have turned to you often, as I flatter myself that yours may have turned to me. You are such a dear friend that I know you will not have forgotten me. And whatever ill you may have heard about me, I trust you did not believe it. I do, however, wish to set the matter straight, and I hope you will not be prejudiced against me when you have heard my story, and that you might even think more kindly of me and we shall be restored to the dear friendship we enjoyed before we were married. I readily acknowledge you made the better choice in this regard.

You will remember that I said, 'I am not romantic' and 'It is better to know as little as possible of the defects of the person with whom you are to pass your life'. How you must have laughed to yourself at my foolish pronouncements, and how you must have pitied me, especially when you knew the felicity of a true union of hearts and minds. In my defence, I will only say that the prospect of being an old maid was an unattractive one, and the means of escape being in Mr. Collins's hand, I grasped it firmly.

At first I was contented enough with my garden and my poultry and my sheep. They gave me ample reward and took up enough of my time to keep me separated from my husband for many pleasant hours. Then there was the anticipation of a happy event, our little 'olive-branch', as my husband liked to say. Indeed, he repeated that phrase so often that I dreaded to hear it, but I bore with him, because I greatly looked forward to that blessing myself. But, as you know, that happiness was not to be, and it was several months before I recovered my health, despite the ministrations of Lady Catherine's physician and my husband's attempts to ensure I ate the milk and egg-yolk porridge and boiled calves' feet recommended by Lady Catherine.

I do not know quite what I should have done, had it not been for the frequent company of my sister Maria, and the intelligent diversions of Colonel Fitzwilliam on the occasions when he visited Lady Catherine at Rosings. They kept me occupied, and gradually my burden lessened and I felt the sadness a little less bitterly. But now I was no longer in the position of a prospective mother, I could not bear my husband's attentions to me. He repeated to me constantly the verses, 'Like arrows in the hands of a warrior are children born in one's youth. Blessed is the man whose quiver is full of them'. A quiver being commonly thought to represent the number five, I could no longer contemplate the sacrifices I would make to achieve it, however much I welcomed the idea of a large family. But after many months, even Mr. Collins tired of shooting his arrows, since no offspring were forthcoming. He did not, however, cease to lecture me on a woman's duty to bear children and run the house, and I was sick to death of the virtuous woman in the book of Proverbs whose price, he assured me ten times a day, was beyond rubies.

I therefore began to cast around for some means of escape. You will know that these means are not many for a woman in my situation, and Mr. Collins, despite his many faults, was a most attentive husband, unwilling to let me out of his sight for very long. I could not, therefore, make prolonged trips home to Lucas Lodge, or to visit you at Pemberley, and any absence would be discoursed on at length by Lady Catherine on my return. You will understand, I know, how I was quite unable to join you in Cambridge, though I wished you well with your endeavours. The best I could hope for was a little excursion to London now and then with Maria.

When we went to the city, we were often in the haberdashers' or linen-drapers' establishments. It gave us both pleasure to examine the shawls and ribbons, and sometimes I would buy Maria a card of lace or a piece of cloth. This gave her a great deal of happiness.

You will remember Maria as an empty-headed young lady, and I am afraid she did not improve after your marriage. She complained often of being bored, and she told me that at home she was frequently overlooked in favour of her younger brothers and sisters, who occupied most of our parents' time. I was therefore not as shocked as I might have been when

I observed her conduct one day at a linen-draper's shop in Cheapside, near the house of your Aunt and Uncle Gardiner, with whom we were staying.

Maria and I spent some time in Mr. Jerome's shop, she examining the shawls and I discussing the prices with his assistant, Mr. Handley. Maria must have looked at twenty to thirty shawls, some with black lace, some with white, others with fringes, but she was not satisfied with any of them. At length we bid Mr. Handley good day and returned to the Gardiners' house. That evening, you may imagine my astonishment when Maria came down to dinner with a new black lace shawl around her shoulders.

'Do you not like it?' she asked. 'It is a perfect match for my dress.'

'I think it is an excellent choice, my dear,' said Mrs. Gardiner. 'I do not think I have seen it before. Did you buy it this afternoon? It is very like the shawls in Mr. Jerome's warehouse.'

Maria looked pleased. 'Oh no, Mrs. Gardiner. It is something I bought in Meryton.'

She tossed her curls and simpered in a way I have seen your sister Lydia do. (I am sorry to allude to this, but you know how Lydia and Kitty and Maria encouraged each other in their behaviour.)

'Indeed?' said Mrs. Gardiner. 'I did not know you were blessed with such an abundant choice of fashions there. I must ask Mrs. Bennet to reserve a shawl for me. It will make an excellent present for Lizzy, next time we visit her in Derbyshire.'

Maria looked a little alarmed, but she carried it well. 'I am afraid this was the last one there, Mrs. Gardiner. Perhaps you will find the same thing here in Cheapside, as you suggest.'

We spent a pleasant evening talking about clothes and fashions in the town and the country. This was not a subject of great interest to the Gardiners or myself, but the young Gardiner girls and Maria enjoyed it, and your uncle and aunt made the topic of greater consequence by discussing the conditions of the labourers who produced the garments and the fabrics. The Gardiners, as you know, are much involved with the work of William Wilberforce, and they opened my eyes to iniquities of which I was hitherto totally unaware. Only think of the good that women such as Lady Catherine could do, if they would use their wealth to further the ends of organisations such as the Anti-Slavery Society.

When we retired to our bedroom, I spoke frankly to Maria.

'That shawl did not come from Meryton,' I said. 'It was not in your trunk when you arrived. Admit it. It came from Mr. Jerome's shop.'

Maria looked uncomfortable, but she did not contradict me.

'He has many shawls, and I only have one, and it is an old one, and this is a new one. He will not miss it.'

I spoke to her very sternly. 'This is not yours. If you take something that does not belong to you, it is stealing.'

She now began to cry and looked very shame-faced. 'I only wanted something for myself. You have Mr. Collins, and my brothers and sisters have our parents. No one wants me.'

I put my arms around her until she had stopped sobbing.

'You are a very silly girl,' I said, 'but you are not a bad girl. We shall take the shawl back to its owner tomorrow.'

Maria looked frightened. 'Will they not arrest me?'

'Why should they?' I asked. 'We shall explain it was a

mistake and we shall pay for the shawl. Then you may keep it.'

'I do not want it now,' she said. But she gave me a very warm hug before we extinguished the candle.

I was in some trepidation when we approached Mr. Jerome's warehouse the next day, but I had confidence we were doing the right thing and nothing untoward would happen to Maria. Mr. Jerome was of an obliging disposition and would be sure to understand our mistake. I would explain how she had picked up the shawl and forgotten to pay for it when we left the shop in haste.

Alas, my confidence was ill-founded. As soon as we entered the establishment with the shawl on my arm, the assistant, Mr. Handley, advanced on us and took us each by the elbow.

'It was these two,' he said. 'Mr. Jerome, I have apprehended them. You must fetch a constable.'

'Sir, I do not know what you mean,' I said.

'Shew me that shawl,' said Mr. Handley.

I placed the shawl on the counter.

'The very one,' he said. 'When I presented you with these shawls yesterday, there were twenty-two. When you left, there were but twenty-one, and yet you did not pay for one.'

'That is true,' I began. 'My sis . . .'

And then I saw how it might look, and thought it wiser not to mention Maria's part.

'That is true,' I continued. 'I took the shawl by mistake. As soon as I realised what I had done, I knew I must return it to you. And here it is.'

Mr. Jerome looked at the shawl. 'And where is the label?'

I was in great consternation, for Maria had removed it.

'It has fallen off, sir.'

'And you have worn the shawl.'

I did not know what to say. It was true the shawl had been worn.

'It was a mistake, sir,' I said. 'I did not mean to wear it. Indeed, I had it on my shoulders only a minute before I realised it was the shawl from your shop, and I knew I must return it as soon as the shop opened.'

Maria was in an agony of anxiety, but I did not look at her, for I did not want her to be accused along with me.

'May my sister be permitted to fetch our friends?' I asked. 'They will assist me.'

'She may go,' said Mr. Jerome. 'But they will not be able to assist you. Here is the constable.'

Mr. and Mrs. Gardiner arrived shortly after, but there was nothing they could do. We paid for the shawl, but Mr. Jerome would not be deterred. After a short session at the Old Bailey, I was sentenced to seven years of transportation.

I hope, my dear Elizabeth, you will not be too greatly shocked by my narrative thus far. Fear not, for the ending is happier.

~

I will not speak of the horrors of the voyage to Australia, or the long months of sickness and deprivation on board ship. The pamphlets the Gardiners gave me to read sustained me somewhat, when I understood I was suffering only a little of what many of my fellow human beings were forced to endure as a matter of course, merely so we could take sugar in our tea. I was also overjoyed on my last night on shore to receive a visit from Mrs. Fry, who gave me and my fellow lady passengers a little package each to occupy us on the voyage, so we could spend our time sewing quilts, which would give us a small income when we sold them on our arrival in Australia.

When I reached New South Wales, I expected to be put to work, and was in much trepidation at what I would find, but I was employed by a gentleman who needed a helper on his poultry farm. He treated me exceedingly well, and I was glad to assist him, not only with the chickens, but also in the kitchen. My life was a hundred times more profitable than it had been at Rosings, and I had the added advantage that I was free of Mr. Collins's irksome presence. My sentence, indeed, had liberated me from the prison I had made for myself, when I was forced into prudence in my younger days. My only regret was that I missed my dear family, and you, my dearest friend.

But my greatest astonishment was yet to come, for after a year in the colony, you may imagine my surprise when my employer announced I had a visitor. I hastened to change my clothes and wash my face and hands. I fear I still had some feathers in my hair when the door opened, and there stood Colonel Fitzwilliam.

'My dear Charlotte,' he said. 'I hoped I should find you here. I have been searching for you high and low.'

'Sir, how did you come here?' I asked, at a loss for words. Had he indeed been searching for me? Or was he here on a tour of duty? If so, I did not see why a British army officer should be in Australia. But then, he was dressed in civilian clothes.

'Pray sit down,' he said, taking me by the hand. 'You are quite pale.'

My employer was discretion itself. He left us and went to attend to the chickens. I sat on the little sofa and Colonel Fitzwilliam sat on the armchair next to me.

'When you left so suddenly,' he said, 'I asked Mr. Collins where you were gone. He told me it was better not to talk of such things, that you had taken ill and were gone abroad, and were not likely to return. I then asked Lady Catherine, but she would not be drawn on the matter.'

'They do not know the whole story,' I said.

'That is what I surmised,' he said. 'And so I spoke to Elizabeth and Darcy. They were equally puzzled, but they said I should ask your family, and so I travelled to Meryton, and though your parents were unwilling to talk to me, Maria was glad to unburden herself at last. She feels your loss keenly, and seemed relieved to tell me the full story. She is full of self-reproach.'

'It is very kind of you, sir,' I said. 'Pray, do not consider my tears. My employer here is very good to me, but he does not know my true history. I dare not tell any one, for fear Maria will be exiled too.'

'I think Maria has learned her lesson,' said Colonel Fitzwilliam. 'She asks only that you return when you can.'

'That is still some years away,' I said. 'And I have nothing to return to. In truth, I am very happy here, apart from the lack of my friends and family.'

I sighed. I felt I had regained a friend only to lose him again, for there was nothing to detain the Colonel here.

'I hope you are pleased to see one friend, at least,' he said, smiling at me.

I had thought him intelligent before, but as I was married to Mr. Collins, I had endeavoured not to notice how very good-looking he was, how wise his countenance, how warm his eyes.

'I am very glad to see one friend,' I replied. 'But I will be sorry when he leaves.'

Colonel Fitzwilliam took my hand. 'I do not intend to leave. I could never afford to marry before, but I have recently become a beneficiary of my uncle's will. It is not a large sum of money, but I have resigned my commission and purchased a tract of land here. I intend to try my hand at farming. And it would be a thousand times better if the farmer had a wife. I wonder, my dear Charlotte, if you would do me the honour of accepting that position? I have loved you for many years, and believe you have long held a deep regard for me, but your marital state prevented us from declaring our feelings. We were both too honourable to risk censure. But now . . .'

My emotions were entirely mixed, as you may imagine.

'Sir,' I said, 'I would be most honoured to accept, but for a small encumbrance—though I feel myself to be free, I am yet married.'

'You are still married in name,' he said. 'But were you ever married in spirit to Mr. Collins?'

'No, I was not,' I admitted. 'And after the loss . . . after my illness, when he at length knew I could bear no more children, we were no longer married at all.'

Here I blushed, but I regarded Colonel Fitzwilliam frankly. I would have no secrets and no falsehood. I wanted him to know all my defects. This was a man worthy of honour and honesty.

'Then, my dearest Charlotte, you would make me the happiest man alive if you would live with me as my . . . unlawfully wedded wife.'

And he took me in his arms and kissed me.

And that, my dear Elizabeth, is my story. Now you know why I am here in Australia, and you know that I have a new husband and a new life. I have for ever rejected the name of Collins. Only you must promise never to tell any one. When the time is right, Colonel Fitzwilliam and I may one day return to England, but for now, we are perfectly contented here. It is a happiness such as I have never known and never expected to know. Many changes have taken place in my life since we last met, but one of the chief among them is this—I can now say with absolute certainty that I, like you, am a true romantic.

Your very affectionate friend,
Charlotte Lucas Fitzwilliam

Chapter 12

Caroline Bingley – A Single Woman

I will admit the idea first came to me at Netherfield, when Elizabeth Bennet arrived to visit her sister. Miss Jane Bennet had foolishly arrived on horseback through a shower of rain, and was wet through. The effect was not lost on my brother, who noted at once how her elegant figure was shewn to greater advantage by her clinging clothes. Of course, she took a cold and her nose turned red, and the effect was undone, but in the case of Eliza Bennet, the opposite was true. When she reached Netherfield after a walk through the fields, her clothes were not wet, but the exertion lent a brilliance to her complexion that soon caught the attention of Mr. Darcy.

I perceived that to partake of exercise in the fresh air was to brighten one's eyes and bring a youthfulness to one's face. And yet, we are not all so lucky as to reside in the country, and there are many ladies in the town who would like to retain, or even enhance, their original good looks. I thought then that a foray into cosmetics would do very nicely to occupy me, until something, or some one, more interesting should arrive.

I had long felt the lack of an occupation, for the balls and dinners and whist parties to which I was accustomed did little to stimulate my mind, and of what use was my material fortune if my mental faculties were doomed to inactivity? Advanced in years as I was, approaching the age of thirty, it was likely I should never find a husband. It is true I had the advantage of a good education at a private seminary, but my social superiority did not allow me to work, and the time often hung heavy on my hands.

I therefore determined, when we returned to London, to seek out an apothecary who would help me recreate the effect of youth, and a certain Mr. Moonshine was willing to oblige. He assured me his concoctions were frequently used by members of the fair sex, as he put it, who were desirous of maintaining their complexions, and he introduced me to a Mrs. Younge, who ran a lodging-house in Edward-street for young ladies who were consumers of his products.

I was much taken by Mrs. Younge. She was a very agreeable woman with a good deal of shrewd business sense. Not at all the kind of person I am accustomed to socialise with, but I was curious about the circles in which she moved, and I thought her boarders might prove to be a ready market to try out our goods. And so it proved. I visited her and met with the young ladies. There was something very *forthcoming* about them, and they were much in the company of soldiers and sailors, whom I frequently passed on the stairs. All of these military men were well dressed and polite, and a good deal more agreeable than my sister's husband, Mr. Hurst.

After a second visit to Mrs. Younge's house, I realised what kind of establishment she kept. To my surprise, this did not turn me against her. Indeed, I was intrigued when she told me she had an additional house in the country, felicitously named Lowhanger Abbey, and that she needed some one educated and *au fait* with the higher ranks of society to manage it. Her hints at my involvement were evident, and I said I would consider the matter.

My first endeavour, however, was to sell cosmetics to the young ladies. I was not, you understand, in *trade*. This was an affair purely for their own benefit, from which I happened to make a little money for my own use. I was pleased that it also opened my mind to the broader world that had remained hidden to me as an educated woman. Mrs. Younge's girls were glad enough to see me, and after several weeks of social intercourse, I came to understand that not all of them were at Mrs. Younge's house of their own volition. Indeed, none of them truly wanted to remain, but they were prevented by poverty and ignorance from leaving and making their own way in the world. Many of them were silly little things, and socially inferior, but I know what it is to be beholden to a man, and I would not be held accountable on their behalf. So I determined I would take on the establishment at Lowhanger Abbey and operate it on different principles. For this purpose, I called on the eldest girl at Mrs. Younge's, Fanny Mount, to assist me. She was a very attractive young lady, dressed in a fetching blue muslin, and with a coy smile that was utterly charming. We had many meetings over tea and crumpets, and after several weeks our plan was ready.

We persuaded Mrs. Younge to give us free rein of the new house and to send with us three of her elder girls, who, I ascertained from Fanny, were the most desirous of leaving Mrs. Younge's employment. Once at the Abbey, the girls were dressed in man's clothes, with high bang-up hats and riding canes, and very fetching they appeared. I then told Mr. Moonshine that Lowhanger Abbey was ready for business and he should send those gentlemen of his acquaintance who were of a less *dominant* frame of mind, who felt themselves to be *naughty* and even in need of *punishment*.

There was no shortage of interest. The first to arrive was an admiral, and Fanny herself took him in charge, once he had paid his fifty guineas. I hid myself in the rear drawing-room and listened. I could not imagine how he could have enjoyed the ensuing application of whips and riding canes, but he emerged an hour later saying she had put on a 'd*** fine shew' and he would return the following Thursday when his wife was out of town.

Fanny and I toasted our first success with a glass of claret.

The next to arrive were two members of parliament and a judge. They were pleased to see our girls in their male attire, but they themselves requested female dress. This was hastily arranged by the expedient of bribing the maids to lend us their clothes. The results were startling to those of us watching from behind the screen, but the men were happy enough, and the judge paid a handsome tip. Mrs. Younge's girls wielded their canes with growing expertise, and every one was happy with the outcome.

At the end of the day, the girls were paid handsomely and returned to London, and Fanny and I toasted our second success.

After this auspicious beginning, our business grew apace. We were soon welcoming a score of gentlemen every day, and our girls were delighted not only to preserve their own bodies, for we made it a condition they would not undress or offer themselves for their clients' use in any way, but to inflict punishment on the male sex, who had done them such harm. Mrs. Younge was ignorant of the manner in which we conducted her business, satisfied only that she was making money. And Fanny and I profited from the transactions too, putting a little aside from each client for our own use, unbeknown to Mrs. Younge. We had worried the price we charged was too high, but the men were willing to pay, and asked only that no one be told of their attendance.

This happy state of affairs continued for several months, until one day we had a visit from a gentleman well known to me. It was Mr. Wickham. I did not deal with him directly, for when I saw him alighting from his curricle I took the opportunity to hide myself in the servants' quarters. It was Fanny who greeted him and brought him into the reception room for a glass of port.

'A d*** fine place you have here,' said he, looking at the distinguished portraits in the entrance hall, and the striped wallpaper. Only part of the house was so furnished, the rest being largely undecorated, but visitors were not allowed to view our hidden quarters.

'Indeed it is, sir,' said Fanny. I praised myself for my astuteness in appointing a girl who had moved in the highest circles before her reduced circumstances led her eventually to Mrs. Younge's establishment. She was uncommonly pretty, and her intelligence was far greater than that of most of our clients. It pains me to say this, but I must admit she had something of Elizabeth Bennet about her. Not that *she* is the epitome of female perfection, but I will admit that when we were at Netherfield her company was not entirely displeasing, and her recent actions in support of women's education are impressive. The procession she organised was very stimulating. Indeed, had it not been for her evident, though covert, fondness for Mr. Darcy when at Netherfield, and his obvious attraction to her, I should have considered admitting her at that time to my circle of friends, though it is true her family left much to be desired. But I could see that Mr. Wickham, who had once shewn a great interest in Elizabeth, was much taken by Fanny.

'I understand from Mrs. Younge this house is one in which a certain number of young ladies are undertaking their studies,' he said.

And here I could see, as I peered carefully around the screen, that he actually winked.

'That is indeed the case,' answered Fanny.

'And do you think you could introduce me to one of these young ladies?' said he.

'Indeed I could, sir. Though their studies are expensive, and we require a contribution to their maintenance.'

'How much is that, pray?'

'It is fifty guineas.'

I could see him give a start. 'Your young ladies must be exceptionally skilled in their art.' And again that wink.

'Exceptionally skilled, sir.'

'Then I will test their skills.'

And he took out his pocket-book and handed her the money.

'I must stipulate, sir, that the young ladies have certain rules. You will find the details on this sheet which you must sign.'

'There.' His pen moved rapidly. 'Now, rules be hanged.' I saw the piece of paper flutter to the floor. 'I am immensely skilled in pleasing young ladies. There is no need to read all this nonsense.'

'As you will, sir. Florence?' She called the prettiest girl, and I could see Mr. Wickham's surprise and, once he had regained his composure, his delight in observing her male attire. 'Florence, would you take our friend to his chamber?'

'Has he been a naughty boy?' asked Florence.

'Very naughty,' said Fanny. 'So naughty that we must tie him up.'

And she produced a pair of handcuffs and proceeded to put them on Mr. Wickham's wrists. That gentleman was so astonished his mouth dropped open and he allowed himself to be led away to the chamber, whence we heard the sound of gentle beating and his increasing fury at the treatment. Well before the hour was over, nay, after only ten minutes, he emerged, still handcuffed, and demanded Fanny return his fifty guineas. She, however, stood firm.

'I am afraid, sir, that we shewed you the rules, and you were fully aware of the treatment you would receive. We have your signature to testify to it.'

'Give me that,' he said, reaching for the paper, but Fanny placed it in a book and gave the book to our gardener, John, a giant of a man whom I had summoned, suspecting trouble from our client. Wickham saw it was useless to protest, but he would not leave without a threat. 'I will tell Mrs. Younge of your conduct,' he said, 'and she will be most unhappy.'

'As you will, sir,' said Fanny.

She removed the handcuffs, and John ushered Mr. Wickham to the front door amid many bitter recriminations from that gentleman.

It was only a few days before Mrs. Younge summoned me. I say "summoned", but I will not be called by any one, least of all a woman of her lowly status, and I went in my own good time.

'I have heard from a friend of mine that Lowhanger Abbey is running in a somewhat unorthodox manner,' she began.

'I do not know what your friend told you,' I said, 'but I have here the signatures of all our gentlemen, and you will see that not one has declined our services.'

She took the sheaf of papers and eagerly searched the names.

'You will notice, too,' I said, 'that you are making money on each transaction, to the sum of seven guineas for each customer.'

'I see,' said she. 'And how much is each customer paying you?'

'Twenty guineas,' said I. 'Ten guineas are for you, six guineas for me, and one each for Fanny and the three girls.'

She sniffed. 'It is very little. I want you to charge more. And see that the girls do all their customers require.'

The next time I went to Lowhanger Abbey, I advised Fanny that we should increase the price. Sixty guineas an hour would permit us to return fifteen guineas to Mrs. Younge. Fanny and I received fifteen guineas each, and the girls received five guineas apiece. The servants and the house maintenance were paid for by Mrs. Younge through an intricate billing system of which she was not aware. By this means, I soon amassed thousands of guineas, and the girls and Fanny were saving to quit the trade and start their lives again as sempstresses. I was surprised at the enjoyment this prospect gave me.

We continued in this fashion for several months, until we had a great misfortune. Our client one afternoon was a bishop. He was desirous of being dressed in purple, and as we could not find a maid's dress of the right colour, he became most unpleasant and commanded us to return his money. When Fanny tried to remonstrate, he knocked her to the ground and said he would report us to the authorities. Then he strode from the house before we could apprehend him.

It was not long before my presence was once more requested by Mrs. Younge. I was not going to be hurried by a woman of such an inferior position, and I took my time before replying, spending several afternoons at whist with my sister and her husband, and ensuring my savings from Lowhanger were safely concealed in my closet. This delay, however, turned out to be my undoing.

It was on the fourth afternoon, just as I was leaving my sister's house, that I was met by a most unsavoury character, who said he had an affair to discuss with me. This objectionable man declared himself to be an attorney, and he made known that I was to appear in court on a certain date, charged with running a bawdy-house. Such an accusation was entirely unmerited, but when I visited Mrs. Younge, her door was closed to me, and I could get no redress from her. One cannot trust the inferior classes, though I must say, Fanny was very strong in my defence, and I promised she should be looked after, whatever the outcome. I had developed a great fondness for her, and she for me. Indeed, our mutual affection was far stronger than I had felt for any man.

And so it was that, some time later, I attended a *meeting* at the Old Bailey. I had heard of Elizabeth and Georgiana's appearance before a judge, and now it seemed it was my turn. I was not in fear for myself. My brother has connections at court and would not suffer me to undergo any indignity. He had never been to the Old Bailey himself, however, and was so far unaware of the matter. I was, moreover, concerned to avoid any form of scandal reaching the ears of Mr. Darcy; and how Elizabeth's mother would crow, should my misfortune be made known to her. Imagine my delight, therefore, when I recognised the judge whom we had entertained on our first day at Lowhanger. His face was a little paler than when we had seen him, and he was breathing even more heavily than when he left us, but I perceived clearly that he also recognised me. He stammered and stuttered throughout the proceedings, and it was but a short time later that I left the court, my name entirely cleared, and the judge mopping his brow in relief that no details of the Lowhanger clients had been divulged.

I returned to my sister's house in a happy state, but was met by a scene of ill-feigned woe. At first I feared my afternoon appointment had been discovered, but my sister informed me that a distant cousin in the West Riding of Yorkshire had died and left us both a substantial fortune. We had never met this cousin, and tears were entirely unnecessary. What is more, my sister had a prejudice against any place north of Stamford and had no desire to travel to Yorkshire. But I had a notion it would suit me very well.

With our cousin's legacy and the money I had saved from my venture with Mrs. Younge, together with my own fortune, I had the means to travel and to purchase a property of my own, and I proposed to Fanny we should remove together to the North of England. She was delighted to accept my invitation. We stopped at Pemberley on the way, and I was not a little surprised to discover my former feelings for Mr. Darcy were now firmly laid to rest. Indeed, from what I had seen of men during my time at Lowhanger Abbey, I no longer desired to be unequally yoked, and was quite content to spend my time without them. Fanny and I journeyed on to York and confirmed our mutual affection by taking communion together at Holy Trinity Church in Goodramgate. We then set about visiting various towns and villages in the North and West Ridings, and were welcomed by a most interesting family named Lister, at Shibden Hall in Calderdale. At their suggestion, Fanny and I travelled on to Hebden Bridge, and it was there I purchased a property that suited us both very well.

We became great friends with Anne Lister, and grew accustomed to life in the country, though both Fanny and I talk often of going to Italy, on Anne's recommendation. I am no longer interested in cosmetics, since the fresh air is sufficient to maintain the bloom in our cheeks. Our estate may be a great deal smaller than Pemberley, but I am sure I am uncommonly happy in my new life with Fanny. As for Mrs. Younge, Mr. Wickham and the bishop, they can go hang. The girls who worked at Lowhanger are in their own employ now, Fanny is with me, and I have finally acknowledged the truth I had long suspected, that a single woman in possession of a good fortune has no want at all of a husband.

Afterword

These stories were written as a light-hearted excursion into possible events occurring after the publication of *Pride and Prejudice*, some of them many years later. I have endeavoured to be accurate in regard to details such as the fashions, furnishings and, particularly, the vocabulary of the period, although I have taken a little poetic licence at times. There are a great many helpful resources for those interested in learning more about Regency England, but the main ones I consulted are listed below.

Many of the ideas for the crimes in these stories are based on real cases recorded in the immensely informative *Old Bailey Proceedings Online, 1674-1913* by Hitchcock, Shoemaker, Emsley, Howard, McLaughlin et al. (Version 9.0, Autumn, 2023). I also recommend Susannah Fullerton's (2005) book *Jane Austen and Crime* for an excellent general overview of criminal activity in the time of Jane Austen,

Claire Tomalin's meticulously researched 2012 biography of Jane Austen furnished me with many useful details of her life. I gleaned other information about practices of the period in Daniel Pool's very entertaining book, *What Jane Austen Ate and Charles Dickens Knew: From Fox-Hunting to Whist – The Facts of Daily Life in Nineteenth-Century England.* Paul Baker's book *Fabulosa!* gave me an insight into the secret language used by certain gay men in the early nineteenth century. The route of Lydia's journey north, and the story of her wilful horse, are based on the Project Gutenberg version of Charles Harper's 1901 book, *The Great North Road: London to York.*

I had thought top hats were common in Jane Austen's time, and indeed there were a large variety of them, but according to the *Oxford English Dictionary* there was no recorded use of the term "top hat" before 1864. I therefore referred to *Lloyd's Treatise on Hats* by Robert Lloyd (1819) on Project Gutenberg, and chose the evocatively named "bang-up" hat instead. It seemed appropriate for Caroline Bingley's story.

Finally, Sally Wainwright's wonderful television series *Gentleman Jack* prompted me to include a reference to Anne Lister.

Several people encouraged me to write these stories. Peter, Jhonessa, Grace, Janet, Laura and Susie, you all supported me in various ways. And in particular, Alan and Joe—you have been an endless source of reassurance and informed feedback. Thank you!